THE NURSE'S CHRISTMAS TEMPTATION

ANN McINTOSH

MILLS & BOON

First published in Great Britain 2019
by Mills & Boon, an imprint of HarperCollins*Publishers*
1 London Bridge Street, London, SE1 9GF

Large Print edition 2020

© 2019 Ann McIntosh

ISBN: 978-0-263-08554-9

MIX
Paper from
responsible sources
FSC™ C007454

This book is produced from independently certified FSC™ paper to ensure responsible forest management. For more information visit www.harpercollins.co.uk/green.

Printed and bound in Great Britain
by CPI Group (UK) Ltd, Croydon, CR0 4YY

Ann McIntosh was born in the Tropics, lived in the frozen north for a number of years, and now resides in sunny central Florida with her husband. She's a proud mama to three grown children, loves tea, crafting, animals (except reptiles!), bacon and the ocean. She believes in the power of romance to heal, inspire and provide hope in our complex world.

Also by Ann McIntosh

The Nurse's Pregnancy Miracle
The Surgeon's One Night to Forever
Surgeon Prince, Cinderella Bride

Discover more at millsandboon.co.uk.

For Tom, Vanessa and Patrick, who've improved my life immeasurably. You helped me grow up more than I helped you!

CHAPTER ONE

AT HER FIRST sight of Eilean Rurie, or Rurie Island, rising like a granite fist from an angry, frothing sea, Harmony Kinkaid gave a satisfied nod.

Rugged black cliffs fronted dismal light green hills wreathed in mist, and the overcast sky was giving everything a sad gray tone. Mizzly rain pattering down on the ferry deck in fits and starts elevated the entire scene to the epitome of dreary.

After the year she'd had, it was the perfect place for her.

Set in the sheltered curve of a sea loch, Eilean Rurie was just far enough from the west coast of Scotland to give Harmony the sense of leaving everything behind. Of course, she had no idea what she was facing once she got there. Being on a somewhat remote island and not knowing anyone would be out of her comfort zone, but she was determined to be up to the task.

The job had come up suddenly, but at just the right time. And when Caitlin, a friend from nursing school, had called out of the blue, Harmony hadn't been able to help thinking it was a sign.

"Hey, I'm in the hospital in Fort William, and I won't be able to go back to work on Eilean Rurie. Can you take over for me until Dr. Mac-Rurie finds a permanent replacement?"

"What's wrong?"

"Preeclampsia. They've put me on bedrest for the duration, and the island's too remote to make it feasible for us to stay there. I know you're in between jobs, and I hoped you'd be willing to fill in for me."

Caitlin was expecting her first child, and Harmony had heard the stress in her usually placid friend's voice. But before she'd been able to reply, Caitlin had continued.

"It's very different from working in London but Cam—Dr. MacRurie—is easy to work for, and there are only about two hundred and fifty people to tend to overall. It would mean being away for Christmas, though..."

Harmony's fingers had tightened on the phone, and she'd hastily swallowed the lump in her throat and replied, "That's all right. Of course I'll do it. I could definitely use the money."

And, even more importantly, it would mean not having to spend the holidays alone in a bare house that had used to be Christmas central.

Before Gran had died, and Mum had decided to take off to Yorkshire with her new man, Fred.

Oh, she wasn't angry about Fred. He was a nice man, and Mum deserved to have a life after devoting hers to looking after Harmony and then Gran too. It had just felt horribly like a betrayal when Mum revealed her holiday plans.

"Fred's got some time off over Christmas, and he wants to spend it with his children and grandchildren. It would be a good time for me to meet everyone, so I've agreed to go."

Harmony had been so shocked and hurt she hadn't even been able to reply.

Mum must have seen her reaction on her face, because she'd quickly added, "You're welcome to come too."

The worry in Mum's tone had brought Harmony back to her senses. "No, Mum. You go and have a great time. I have a few applications out there, and I'm going to want to be on hand if anyone calls me to come in for an interview."

Yet inside it had felt like the last straw in an awful year. First her two-year relationship with Logan had ended, and only a couple of months later Gran had passed away unexpectedly, leaving Mum and Harmony heartbroken. Her mother's mother had lived with them since her dad had died, when Harmony was only six, and had been an integral part of their little family.

Then, as if those things weren't enough, Harmony's boss of six years had decided to retire. Although the staff had been assured their jobs were secure, one of the first things the new GP had done was let them all go.

When Mum had dropped her bombshell Harmony had been totally set adrift. She didn't like change. Life had been fine the way it was, and now suddenly it was all upside down. The loss of their traditional mother/daughter Christmas in particular had left her in a tailspin.

She felt as though everyone and everything she cherished about the season was gone, and all she could anticipate was loneliness. Just thinking about it made her eyes watery.

But maybe saying to heck with Christmas and having the enforced alone time that was ahead was exactly what she needed. Getting away from the familiar to really think about where she wanted to go in life.

From all she'd heard and read about small communities like this one, she wouldn't be surprised if it took a lot longer than she would be around for people even to warm to her. That suited her just fine. Peace and quiet were what she was looking for. Although it would be lonely living by herself for the first time, and in a new environment to boot, it would also be the best opportunity to contemplate her next move.

"Your first trip to Eilean Rurie?"

The deckhand's voice pulled her out of her sour thoughts, and she blinked to chase away the silly tears before they fell.

"Yes," she said, as the ferry rounded the end of the island and headed to what she assumed was the port.

"Bit drab looking right now, but it'll be better in a few days."

"What happens in a few days?" she asked. But he had already hurried off—no doubt to prepare for docking.

Other than a magical transportation of the island to a tropical location, Harmony couldn't think of anything that would make it look better. The town and dock area continued the gray-on-gray theme, although she had to admit that had more to do with the overcast day than anything else. Most buildings were either whitewashed or cream-colored stone, and the overall effect was of a somewhat quaint, old-fashioned village.

The cry of sea birds and the sound of the wind along with the brisk, damp air was strangely invigorating, and Harmony felt a little surge of excitement. This peaceful place, far from the rush and noise of London, would surely be perfect for the quiet contemplation she needed to figure out her future.

The serene effect was shattered by a *whoosh* that was easily heard over the ferry engines, and the sight of a man rocketing up from the water. It took Harmony a couple of confused seconds to realize he was wearing a water jet-pack, which had propelled him high into the air. As she watched he swooped down, then started twisting and turning close to the surface of the loch, doing stunts.

She couldn't decide whether or not riding the contraption was crazier than going into the no doubt freezing water but, however she cut it, he was clearly out of his gourd. Horrified and fascinated all at once, she stood watching his performance as the ferry moved closer to shore.

He shot high into the air again and then, in an instant, plummeted toward the water. Harmony wanted to close her eyes, so she wouldn't see him die, but couldn't look away, covering her mouth to curtail the shriek of fear rising in her throat. Somehow, seemingly inches from the water, he got the spluttering jetpack back under control and rose again.

She turned away, her hands shaking, pretending to fuss with her luggage so no one would realize how scared she'd been.

Why did people do these daredevil things? Didn't they realize how dangerous it was? That they could lose their lives doing that kind of nonsense?

Anger superseded her fear, and she mentally cursed the man who'd upset her just before she was supposed to meet her new boss. Her heart was pounding, her shoulders were up around her ears, and her stomach roiled. Taking a deep breath, she forced herself to relax as best she could.

Taking out her compact, she slicked on a little lipstick and, noticing the stress lines between her brows, forced herself to release as much tension as possible.

A little calmer as the ferry approached the dock, she glanced down at the shore, trying to see if she could pick out Dr. MacRurie. There was one elderly man there, but Harmony was sure he wasn't the doctor, who Caitlin had said was in his thirties. Hopefully he hadn't forgotten she was arriving today, although no doubt she could find her own way to the surgery and the apartment above it where she was staying. The village wasn't that big, after all.

Glancing at her watch, she realized the ferry was actually a few minutes early. The doctor was probably on his way—unless there'd been a medical emergency somewhere.

Without thought she let her gaze track back to where the man with the jetpack had been, and found him wading out onto the shingles alongside the loch. Even from a distance she could see he was in amazing shape, with the wetsuit clinging to muscular thighs, bum, and torso.

Suddenly, as though sensing her interest, he turned and looked back at the ferry. It would be impossible for him to make her out from that distance, but still she ducked away, embarrassed for no good reason. Nothing wrong or illegal about admiring a man's backside—especially when he couldn't see you doing it. And she did love a good backside...

Hopefully he was just a visitor to the island and she wouldn't have to interact with him. That way she wouldn't be tempted to tell him how crazy she thought he was, doing what he'd been doing. Besides, even if she hadn't been turned off by his daredevil stunt, good looking men were on her no-no list right now.

Her experience with Logan had been lesson enough. She'd thought him the perfect fit for her: a handsome yet staid and sensible Certified Public Accountant with a solid head on his shoulders. At least that was what she'd thought until he'd told her he was in love with an intern at his office and was giving up his job to move to Australia with her and start an Out-back tour company.

She'd been totally gobsmacked, in equal parts desperately hurt and angry.

Her mum had seemed sympathetic, but un-surprised, while her gran had said, "He's too boring anyway."

But Logan's lack of excitement was one of the things she'd liked best about him. The last thing she wanted in her life was someone like Dad, whose recklessness and need for adven-ture had gotten him killed on a mountain that, because of his health concerns, he should never have been climbing. She wanted someone safe, reliable, who wouldn't break her heart or leave her to struggle on her own to raise their child the way her mum had had to.

Maybe she was better off on her own long term, anyway. Loving others just brought pain as far as she could tell.

As the ferry docked, Harmony put her bale-ful thoughts aside to heft her tote bag onto her shoulder, then pull up the handle of her wheeled suitcase. Taking another deep breath, she set off for the gangplank, ignoring the flutters of anxiety in her stomach.

Somewhere along the line she'd come to the conclusion that life went on, and that what happened was out of her hands. All she could control was how she faced it, and this new job, in this strange place, was to be met head-on, and with a certain amount of panache, to make up for her fear of the unknown.

Pausing to let an older lady go ahead of her, Harmony ran her hand over the faux fur collar of her favorite tweed trench coat, letting the softness of the fabric soothe her jangling nerves. She'd thought about wearing more casual clothes, but dismissed the impulse. Just because her new job was on an island it didn't mean she wanted to arrive looking as though she didn't take it seriously. Besides, she liked nice clothes; she felt more confident when she was well dressed.

With her head determinedly high, Harmony went down the gangplank to the dock. When no one stepped forward to meet her, she kept walking toward the building marked "Dock Master's Office" for all the world as though she knew where she was going.

Suddenly four older ladies, whom she'd thought were there to meet the woman she'd let go down the gangplank ahead of her, surrounded her, bringing her progress to a screeching halt.

"Nurse Kinkaid?" one of them asked with a smile. "You *are* Nurse Kinkaid, aren't you?"

"Yes."

"Oh, wonderful! Isn't it wonderful, girls?"

Unsure about what was so wonderful, Harmony made no comment, simply plastered a smile on her face as all the women seemed to be speaking at once.

"So lovely to have you!"

"Are you Scottish?"

"What a looker you are!"

"Do you craft?"

"How old are you?"

"I adore your coat!"

Stunned by the barrage, Harmony let go her suitcase and held up her hands, one of which had her umbrella in it. Three of the ladies fell silent and stepped back in unison. The fourth stood her ground, the smile on her face never faltering.

"Don't mind those chatterboxes, Nurse Kinkaid. A bunch of magpies, they are."

She held out her hand and Harmony instinctively took it, receiving a hearty handshake.

"I'm Eudora Moxley, but call me Dora. And these old bags are Ingrid, Sela and Kat."

"Katherine," the tallest of the others growled.

"Kat's a little touchy about her name, but don't let it worry you. It's the English coming out in her."

"For goodness' sake, Eudora." The other woman huffed. "I've lived here for nigh on thirty years. Don't I merit being Scottish by now?"

"You got here thirty years too late for that, Kat," one of the other women interjected, although whether it was Ingrid or Sela, Harmony had no idea. All the women except for Katherine tittered.

"That's enough of that," Katherine retorted. "The nurse is going to think we're loopy."

"Oh, but we are—and best she knows it from day one," Dora retorted, giving Harmony's fingers one last squeeze before finally releasing them. "We're the Crafty Islanders, in charge of—well…almost everything here on Eilean Rurie. We wanted to be on hand to greet you and welcome you to the island."

"Thank you," Harmony replied weakly, still somewhat shell-shocked by what they called a greeting but felt more like a mugging. "Do you have any idea where I might find Dr. Mac-Rurie?"

"Oh, he'll be along any minute now. The Laird is always on time, and the ferry was early."

"Laird?" Wasn't that Scottish for some kind of a peer? Caitlin hadn't mentioned anything about him being a peer.

"That's just a nickname, dear," Katherine said. "Although he does own most of the island, Cam's not one to stand on ceremony. It's not like he's a duke or anything like that."

"There you go. That's why you're not Scottish yet, Kat." Dora smirked. "Laird is far better than Duke any day."

"Tosh" was the testy reply. "You've no idea what you're talking about."

And they started in on each other again, leaving Harmony's head swimming as insults and ripostes flew back and forth.

If these ladies really did run the place, how did they get anything done? Whether they would impact her ability to do her job was another question she really wanted answered too. As assisting nurse and office manager, she'd brook no interference in her work.

"Ladies," she said, loudly enough to cut through the arguing, and was relieved when they all stopped and looked at her. "It was lovely meeting you, but if you would just point me in the right direction…?"

"No need," Dora said, beaming at something behind her. "Here comes the Laird now."

Instinctively Harmony turned, looked, but all she saw was the guy in the wetsuit coming up along the sea wall. No one else.

Then it struck her—hard.

Her new boss was the handsome jetpack daredevil with the nice bum.

Oh, no.

CHAPTER TWO

CAM WAS STILL buzzing with adrenaline from the jetpack as he made his way up from the beach along the path on the seawall. It had been such a rush he'd ridden it for longer than he'd planned, and had missed his chance to change before meeting the ferry. Hopefully his new nurse would be the easygoing type, and wouldn't be fazed by meeting her new boss when he was wearing a wetsuit.

It was a shame he hadn't been able to give Sanjit permission to offer water jetpack rides to visitors, but he'd had to nix the idea even though Sanjit had put up a good argument.

"It could be a new draw for visitors in summer, when we have our slump. Another activity to add to the website, making a trip here more attractive at times other than Christmas."

"True, but the liability issue is one we can't get away from." He'd slapped the younger man on the shoulder, then reached for his towel. "It's a lot of fun, but one major accident and the entire island would suffer the consequences."

It was true. Because the MacRurie Trust owned most of Eilean Rurie, no matter what insurance Sanjit might purchase to cover operating a water jetpack rental, the trust—and Cam as its director—would still be considered liable should anything go wrong. One major lawsuit might break the bank, or at least severely deplete it. He considered the island to be entrusted to him for posterity, so protecting it and its inhabitants was his first order of business.

But, wow, it had been tempting to give Sanjit the go-ahead—if for no other reason than being able to ride the jetpack himself.

Approaching the dock, he saw the Crafty Islanders had beat him there, and had a well-dressed woman he assumed was his new nurse and administrator surrounded. She seemed to be fending them off with her umbrella—a sight which made Cam snort, as he tried to hold back laughter.

Not that he blamed Nurse Kinkaid in the slightest. The CIs *en masse* were a force to be reckoned with. There was no doubt in his mind they were peppering her with intrusive questions and firing off comments before she could even decide whether to answer or not. That was their usual *modus operandi*, and they could frighten the stoutest of souls.

"Please don't scare off my lifesaver," he muttered, picking up his pace, hoping to break up the interrogation before it got too bad.

Then the young woman looked over her shoulder, her thick, curly hair swinging away from her face as she did so. Her gaze tracked past Cam, then snapped back to him, and her eyes widened.

Cam, midstride, had to catch himself so he didn't falter under what he could only describe as the glare she sent him.

But even with lines between her eyebrows and her lips pursed into a disapproving rosette, she was gorgeous. He had only a moment to register her high cheekboned face and skin like golden syrup mixed with cinnamon before she turned back around, but the effect lingered.

Something about the curve of her cheek and chin, the long line of her throat, gave him a jolt of adrenaline on top of the residue already keeping his nerves jangling. It had been a very long time since the sight of a woman had brought him to total awareness, filling him with curiosity and inciting the kind of physical interest he least expected, or wanted.

Since leaving his job with a refugee agency four years before, and taking over the management of Eilean Rurie, he had made the island his base. The transition to being in one place after travelling the world had been difficult, but in a strange way it had afforded him the chance to do more of the adventurous activities he enjoyed.

He had time to travel now, to climb, cave, to do whatever else he wanted, and he was having the time of his life. There was no room in his life for the kind of visceral fascination he felt with just one glimpse of this young woman.

It would be okay, he reassured himself as he finally neared the group. She wouldn't be around for very long. He just had to get through the Christmas rush, and then he could find a permanent replacement. Ignoring this strange attraction wouldn't be too hard.

"There you are—finally," Dora said.

"You'll be late for your own funeral," Sela added.

"The later the better. But I'll have you know I'm exactly on time," Cam retorted, giving his watch a pointed glance before turning to the silent young woman and holding out his hand. "Nurse Kinkaid, I presume?"

"You presume correctly," she replied, seeming to hesitate for a moment before taking his outstretched hand and giving it a brief, firm shake. "And I understand you're Dr. Mac-Rurie?"

Her eyes were gorgeous. Hazel, fringed with dark, tightly curled lashes, they matched her skin tone and gave her the look of a haughty lioness. Her watchful gaze, coupled with the low, husky voice made his toes curl.

Taken aback, especially by his reaction to her, all he could manage to say was "In the flesh."

"You mean in the wetsuit, don't you?" Ingrid asked, making all the CIs snicker.

Suddenly aware of his state of undress—which hadn't bothered him in the slightest before—Cam frowned, making them all giggle harder. Nurse Kinkaid didn't join in, but the little lines between her brows quickly came and went.

"Yes, well… If you'll come with me to the

Dock Master's Office, Nurse Kinkaid, I'll change and take you over to the surgery."

"So, did you give Sanjit the approval to run his new business?" Katherine interjected, before he could make his escape.

"Unfortunately, no."

"Liability?" asked Ingrid, who was a retired barrister, and Cam nodded.

"Got it in one." Before any of them could get going again, he quickly added, "Let me take your suitcase, Nurse Kinkaid, and we'll be on our way."

As he matched actions to words the CIs chorused their goodbyes, peppered with lovely-to-meet-yous and we'll-catch-up-soons, all aimed at the new nurse—who, wisely, exited their orbit with just a friendly wave and the slight upturning of her lips.

"Will we see you at the planning meeting this evening, Cam?" called Dora.

"Of course," he called back, making sure not to break stride in case they took it as an invitation.

"Wow," the nurse said, as soon as they were out of earshot. "They're something, aren't they?"

"That they are," Cam said, but was suddenly protective of the women who often drove him bonkers. "But, despite being a pain in my rear most of the time, they're invaluable to the island. With such a small population it's good to have people willing to get involved and organize things."

"I'm sure. However, I hope that doesn't apply to your practice? I find I work best with only one boss. Causes far less confusion."

"Good Lord, no." Cam actually laughed at the thought of the CIs butting into his real work.

He opened the door to the Dock Master's Office, and stood back for her to enter ahead of him.

"They're involved with practically all other aspects of life on the island, though, just so you know."

"I can see that being the case."

She'd stepped through the door ahead of him and Cam found himself admiring her figure, which was full and curvy. Lush hips swayed with a siren's rhythm as she walked, mesmerizing him until he caught himself and resolutely tore his gaze away.

Even more aware of the wetsuit, and feeling

silly in the face of his new, rather formal nurse, Cam said, "If you'll wait here, Nurse Kinkaid, I'll get changed as quickly as possible and take you to your apartment."

"Please, call me Harmony," she said, while looking around the office. Seemingly without conscious thought, she straightened a pile of magazines on the table beside the door. "When I hear 'Nurse Kinkaid' like that, I instinctively look around for my mother."

"Sure," he said, seeing an opening to get to know her better but unable to take advantage of it. She completely unsettled him, making him want to get away and catch his breath, not to mention get out of his wetsuit. "I'll remember that. Be right back."

But as he shimmied out of the wetsuit he found himself wondering what she'd look like if she truly smiled. Something told him that rather prim mouth would turn sumptuous and appealing.

Become eminently kissable.

Cam cursed to himself.

She's definitely going to be a problem.

He just had to make sure that, no matter what happened, the problem didn't involve him.

The interest she stirred in him wasn't something he'd ever consider acting on. Even if getting involved with an employee wasn't tacky—which it was—he liked his relationships short and with no strings attached. No matter how quickly her tenure on the island would be over he'd have to work with her, and the chances of it all going sideways were large.

Finally dressed in his street clothes, he grabbed his jacket and went back out into the main part of the office. Danny Smith, the Dock Master, wasn't there, so Harmony was still alone, standing in front of one of the myriad pictures on the wall. It was a painting of one of the rescue boats that used to be launched from the island in rough seas back in the early part of the twentieth century.

"That's my great-grandfather in the prow of that boat," he said, going to stand beside her. "They were probably going out to help with a sea rescue after a wreck—or at least that was what the artist was portraying."

She sent him a brief glance, and once more he felt a zing of electricity when he realized her eyes were more green than gold. Getting used to them was going to take some doing.

"Do you still have a lifeboat station here?" she asked.

"I wish," he said.

How many times had he stood staring at this painting, imagining himself on that boat, fighting the seas, on his way to save lives?

"Now the Coast Guard handles all the rescues. In the old days almost all the islands had manned boats, because it took the authorities much longer to get to the site of a wreck. Now, once someone radios the helicopters can be in the air in a matter of minutes. The private rescue units aren't needed anymore. I think the last one was disbanded here in the nineteen-seventies."

"Hmm."

It was a noncommittal sound, and he figured the conversation was over. "Shall we head over to the surgery?"

"Sure," she said, but she stared at the painting a little longer before turning away.

He led her out through the other side of the building, which took them onto the main street through the village. This time of the afternoon, there weren't many people around, but he knew many of the residents were peeping out from behind their curtains. Everyone knew the nurse was arriving today. Everyone was curious.

As they walked he pointed out the Post Office, the grocery store, the pub, and Sanjit's restaurant, thinking them the most important.

"The Ladies from Hades?" she said, obviously catching sight of the pub sign, with a kilted and armed Highlander painted on it.

"It's a play on the nickname for a famous Scottish regiment."

"The Black Watch," she said, surprising him. "Must have been opened by an ex-military man. And you have a curry shop here too?"

He wanted to ask how she knew about the Black Watch and their World War I nickname, but left it for another time.

"We're actually very lucky," he explained, speaking a little louder than usual because of the sound of her suitcase bumping along behind him over the cobbles. He'd left the sliver of sidewalk to her and her high heels, since the last thing he needed was for her to twist her ankle before she even started working. "Eilean Rurie has attracted a variety of artists, farmers, and business people over the years, making our population rather more eclectic than some of the other islands."

"Like the owner of the curry shop?"

"Exactly. Sanjit Gopaul came here on vacation with his parents and, for whatever reason, fell in love with the island. He came back and asked if I'd be willing to let him open a restaurant, and I said sure. That was five years ago. He's been an amazing addition to the island and shows no signs of wanting to leave. In fact, he also runs a canoe rental and tour operation during the summer, and he's always looking for new businesses to start."

"Including that jet thing?"

There was no mistaking the disapproval in her voice, and his look at her profile found it echoed there in her pursed lips. It made Cam's hackles rise a bit.

"Yes, like the water jetpack. I was sad to have to tell him no. It was a lot of fun. Wouldn't you like to have a go?"

She gave him a bland look, all censure erased from her expression. "I should say not. I'm not into that kind of thing."

Striving for a light tone, he teased, "What kind of thing? Having fun?"

Looking into the window of the shop they were passing, she replied, "More like stuff that'll get you killed or maimed."

"Ha! It's safe as houses if you're careful and know what you're doing."

The skeptical look she gave him scorched him to his toes.

"No wonder you didn't give him permission to offer it to visitors." Then, as if tired of the discussion, she changed the subject completely. "Your village is beautiful—although I'll admit when I first saw the island from the ferry I thought it looked like something out of a very scary story."

That made Cam chuckle, even though he still felt the sting of her retort about the jetpack. He knew the exact vista she was talking about.

"Eigg Point, no doubt—before you round the headland and see the village. That sheer black cliff with the sea foaming around its base does look like it belongs in a horror movie on a misty, overcast day like today. On a sunny day, though, when the hills are so startlingly green they look like they were drawn with crayon and the water is smooth and clear, it's very different. There's the surgery," he added, pointing across the grassy village green to the three-story building beyond.

"That's your surgery? It looks more like a fancy hotel!"

Cam chuckled. "My great-grandfather built it to try and attract a decent doctor to take up residence. I used to tease my grandfather that he only took up medicine so he'd be able to work in the second nicest building on the island. He didn't deny it."

"I don't blame him," she said.

The appreciation in her voice was pleasing.

"Normally I'd cut across the green to get to the surgery, but it's pretty wet right now and your heels would sink in."

"Thank you."

She had a prim way of speaking he rather liked, and an intriguing way of pronouncing some words that gave unusual flavor to an otherwise very North London voice. Caitlin had mentioned that Harmony's mother's family had originally come from Jamaica, and he thought he could hear an echo of that migration in the nurse's voice. It was so nice, especially with its husky tone, he was tempted to keep her talking so he could go on hearing it.

"Patients come in through either the front door or the one closest to the car park on the north side," he told her as they approached the surgery. "But you have your own entrance on the other side."

Cam led her around the building, and as they got to the door heard her give a little gasp.

"Oh! What's that back there?"

She was looking up the hill through the trees, along the track he used every day.

"That's the nicest building on the island— Rurie Manor."

Big hazel eyes stared at him. "You live there?"

"Yeah," he said, opening the outer door and holding it for her, once more pleased at her awestruck reaction to his home. "But only in a small part of it. Most of the Manor is a hotel now."

Harmony turned back to stare at the Manor a moment more, before stepping through the door and into the entryway.

Cam glanced at his watch. Time to test his glucose levels.

Handing her the keys, he said, "There's another door at the top of the stairs, and the door behind me leads into the surgery, so I sometimes come in this way, but otherwise you'll be the only person using it. Go on up and check out your apartment, and I'll bring up your suitcase in a moment."

"Thank you."

Her slightly stiff reply made him want to break the ice a little more. He was used to a relaxed atmosphere in his practice and hoped to establish that type of working relationship with her too. Even with his niggling suspicion he should actually keep her as distant as he could. Just standing in the small entryway she seemed too close, with her citrusy perfume warming the air between them and those golden eyes surveying him with solemn intensity.

"Hopefully life on the island won't seem too tame and boring for you after living and working in London. At least Christmas should be exciting."

His words stumbled to a halt, arrested by the flash of pain crossing her face.

"I'm looking forward to the quiet," she said, turning toward the steps and hitching her tote bag higher. "And Christmas can pass me by and I won't complain."

Had he somehow put his foot in his mouth?

He couldn't see how. Everyone loved Christmas, didn't they?

But even as he was trying to figure out what he'd said wrong he found himself staring once more at her delectable rear end, until it sashayed around the corner of the landing and disappeared.

CHAPTER THREE

HARMONY STOOD IN the middle of the apartment, not even taking in the space around her, annoyed at herself for being so curt with her new employer. Not to mention for the sarcastic comment she'd made to him earlier about the water jetpack.

It wasn't really like her to be that way, but hearing him make light of her innate dislike of risky behavior had irked her—so, like her mother always said, she'd run her mouth, speaking before thinking.

But there was something about him that had put her on edge from the first time she'd looked him in the eyes. He was, she had to admit, a fine specimen. Handsome, in a rugged, outdoorsy kind of way, with brown hair just shy of ginger and blue-gray eyes, his looks alone made him a standout. Couple his face with a body that looked amazing even in a wetsuit, and Harmony knew he must make women's heads turn faster than wheels on ice.

But it wasn't his looks that were making her snarky. There was an air about him—an aura of confidence and ease that, conversely, made her tense and jumpy. And when he'd mentioned Christmas, just as she'd promised herself a hiatus from the entire season, it had brought all her pain flooding back.

For almost as long as she could remember Christmas had been a special time for Mum, Gran and Harmony. There was always a flurry of baking, both English treats and Jamaican. And a night specially planned to trim the tree while listening to a variety of holiday music or old movies.

They'd also watch *Greetings from Yaad*, an hour-long special filmed in Jamaica, in which people could wish their loved ones in England a Merry Christmas. Harmony had used to dislike the amateurishly filmed show, until Gran had said, "We may not know any of these people, but it makes me happy to hear the accents of my youth."

That had always led to conversations about old times in Jamaica, and even how things had been for Gran when she'd first moved to England. She'd been part of the Windrush generation, coming from the colonies to help with the rebuilding efforts in the UK after World War II. She'd had to leave all her family behind, including Mum, but once she'd gotten herself a job and somewhere to live she'd started saving so she could send for her husband and daughter.

Grandpa had decided he didn't want to live in England, so eventually Mum had travelled to the UK with her Uncle Shorty, Gran's brother. Uncle Shorty, a perennial bachelor, had settled in Birmingham, but had come to visit every Christmas until he died, adding to the family fun. Harmony could still remember his plaid driving cap, his booming laugh and the way the scent of smoke and cologne clung to his clothes.

On Christmas Eve they'd have neighbors and friends in and out of the house, each one of them bringing a little gift, receiving goodies in return.

Until they'd passed away her other grandparents had come too, on Christmas morning, even after Dad hadn't been there anymore, and all Harmony remembered was the joy and closeness. The laughter and sometimes a few shared tears too.

All that was gone now—and darn Dr. Mac-Rurie for reminding her of what she'd lost this year.

But it wouldn't do to start their working relationship off on a bad footing, and she wondered if it would be politic to apologize to him for her behavior.

Harmony considered that option, then dismissed it. Unless he brought it up, she wouldn't either. Less said, soonest mended, right?

Suddenly realizing she was in danger of having the doctor come up and find her still standing there like a ninny, Harmony quickly took off her coat and shoes, stowing them in the entryway closet. Then she took a really good look around.

The apartment was a lot larger than she'd expected, with an L-shaped living and dining room and a kitchen almost as big as her mum's. There were also not two but three good-sized bedrooms, all tastefully decorated with a combination of new and more traditional furniture. And the bathroom, with its deep soaker tub and a separate shower, made her coo.

The entire space had obviously been modernized, but whoever had done it had been careful to keep a lot of the original Victorian elements. The living room fireplace, which was lit, had the most amazing carved mantel and pillars, along with a tile surround and hearth. There were medallions on the ceiling, and intricately carved jambs around the doors. Even the door knobs were decorative, and Harmony found herself smiling as she palmed one of the floral patterned porcelain ovoids.

She staked out the bedroom she wanted, which had a sleigh bed and large windows that were letting in the last of the afternoon light. Outside was a tiny balcony, just big enough for a miniscule wrought-iron table and matching chair, and in the distance was Rurie Manor, sitting in solitary splendor on the top of a gently sloping hill.

It looked gorgeous, and she wondered if she'd get a chance to see the inside. Although if it had been turned into a hotel, she might be disappointed.

Hearing Dr. MacRurie coming up the stairs, she went back into the living area just as he came through the front door.

"Here you go," he said, putting down her suitcase, seemingly not at all put out by her ill-mannered behavior. "Have you decided which room you want? I'll put your case on the luggage stand for you."

"Thank you. That one," she said, pointing to the still open door, determined to put her best foot forward.

He wheeled the suitcase across the living area, speaking as he went. "I hope you'll be comfortable here. Caitlin and her husband had a dog, so I gave them a cottage instead—for convenience. Knowing you'd have to be here over the holidays, I figured this place is big enough that if you have someone come for Christmas they can stay with you."

There he went with the whole Christmas thing again!

"I won't." It came instinctively, pain pushing the brusque words out. Drawing herself up, and not wanting to sound as churlish as she felt, she added, "But thank you."

"Oh." He'd put her bag in the room and was standing in the doorway, his gaze sharp. But all he said was "Well, if that changes you'll be all set. But if not at least you won't be bored. This time of year is nice and busy."

"This time of year? What's so special about it?"

Giving her a surprised glance, he said, "Caitlin didn't tell you?" Then he answered his own question. "Of course, she had other things on her mind. Eilean Rurie is famous for its Winter Festival. Well, it used to be called the Christmas Festival until the eighties, when my grandfather changed the name. We're called the North Pole of Scotland, and we attract hundreds of people every year."

Oh, come on.

"You're kidding, right?"

"Nope."

He gave her one of his killer smiles, and Harmony's stomach fluttered, making her look away in case her reaction showed.

"Did you know that celebrating Christmas—well, really it was Yule back then—was banned in Scotland in the sixteenth century? Christmas Day wasn't made a public holiday until 1958, and Boxing Day was only recognized in the seventies. My great-grandfather decided he wanted to make the holidays a big splash, and encouraged all the islanders to do it too, once the ban was officially lifted. It evolved into the Christmas Festival, and then the Winter Festival, and it's grown with each year."

Plunking herself down onto the squishy sofa, Harmony only just stopped herself from putting her head in her hands in disbelief. Hundreds of people, running around singing carols and doing who knew what else?

Just shoot me now!

Yet the smile on the doctor's face told her there was only one of them in the room who viewed the upcoming festivities with horror. The happy anticipation on his face spoke volumes, and it made Harmony pull herself together once more, even while wondering how many other times this man was going to throw her off-kilter.

"How on earth do you accommodate hundreds of people here? The village doesn't look big enough."

"Well, the manor has a lot of rooms, and most of the villagers offer bed and breakfast services, using their spare rooms, or even small apartments attached to their houses. Most of the temporary staff are island kids coming back for winter break, but the others who don't have a place to stay have dormitories behind the church. A couple of really entrepreneurial souls have even put up a few tiny houses on their properties, and rent those out to visitors. We also get quite a few daytrippers, and the ferry runs more frequently to accommodate them. Most of the residents benefit in some way from the festival. If they didn't we wouldn't bother. It's a lot of work."

Harmony shook her head in disbelief, still not sure he was telling the truth. "But there's nothing going on. No one's putting up lights or decorating."

"It's too early," he said, somewhat cryptically, then added, "Poke around downstairs tomorrow, if you like, or just rest up from your trip. The surgery is closed on Saturday afternoon, and Sunday, although everyone on the island has my number and will call if they need me. I've made a list of numbers and left it on the hall table for you, in case you need anything, and the CIs have stocked the fridge—although, who knows what they put in there? Ingrid's a vegan, and Katherine's always on some kind of diet, Dora has a sweet tooth that won't quit, and Sela is crazy for cheese."

By the time he'd finished his recitation Harmony found herself chuckling. "I'm sure I'll be able to make a meal of whatever they've left, and I'll bless Dora forever if there's a chocolate something in amongst the rest."

Cam was grinning too. "I have no doubt there is, but if you feel up to it nip over to the pub too. They do a really great Scotch pie on Saturdays."

"Maybe I will," she said.

"Right, well… I have to go. Final planning meeting tonight, and it will no doubt be a fractious one. When we get to this time of year they usually are, because everyone is so frazzled and behind on everything. If you need anything give me a shout. I always have my phone on me."

He paused halfway out through the door.

"Oh, and there's an Armistice Day ceremony at the cenotaph on Monday, starting at ten. Come along, if you'd like."

Then he was gone, clattering down the stairs, leaving her to wonder why, when she had been so determined to stay away from Christmas, she'd landed in the North Pole of Scotland. And why, having decided to ignore men, she found her boss so damned handsome.

Cam had been right about the meeting being contentious, but he couldn't seem to keep his mind on the grumbles and arguments going on around him. Instead he found himself thinking about his new nurse. Her sometimes curt way of speaking, juxtaposed with her delightful throaty giggle as he listed the CIs eating habits, made her a fascinating enigma. And, yes, her delicious looks.

Even though he wasn't interested in relationships he was still all-male—able and willing to appreciate a beautiful face and a lovely curvy figure. As long as he remembered he could look but not touch, it was all good.

"Melanie, the theme was decided back in February. It's not our fault if you've not gotten on board with it."

At the sound of Dora's firm rebuttal Cam pulled his thoughts away from Harmony Kinkaid and back to the battle of wills going on in front of him.

"But it's silly. We did Love as a theme before. Why do it again?"

Melanie was as stubborn as ever, and as one of Scotland's best-known living potters always felt her word should be law. But Dora never fell in line with that concept.

"That was nigh on twenty years ago. And what better theme could we have for the Winter Festival than that? No matter the religion, or the holiday, love is at the center of them all, isn't it?"

Cam intervened, before things got too heated.

"Melanie, you know full well it's too late to change the theme, so either you've gone with it or not. The choice was yours."

Then Hugh Jacobson had a complaint about the decision to extend the festival hours to ten at night. "The strain on the electricity grid will increase, along with the costs. I don't subscribe to this."

Cam doubted that was his real reason for complaining. Hugh was probably worried that the extra noise and lights would disturb his mother, but didn't want to come right out and say so.

"Hugh, the new wind turbine provides more

than enough power to cover the additional load, and the generators were serviced last month. The increased revenue for us all will more than offset any additional costs, so I'm sure we'll be fine."

"But the noise…the lights on until so late. It's untenable."

"I'll buy you some blackout curtains when I go to the mainland next Wednesday," Sela interjected, and although Hugh still looked unhappy the meeting moved on.

Afterwards Cam realized he wasn't the only one thinking about Nurse Kinkaid—although, perhaps not in the same way.

"I thought your new nurse might have come to the meeting. She looks as though she'd be a good addition to the planning team" was Dora's opening sally.

The last thing Cam wanted was to spend more time with Harmony Kinkaid than necessary. His unsettling reaction to her made keeping her at arm's length a good thing. Besides, every time he'd mentioned Christmas she had withdrawn at the talk of the season.

But there was no way he was letting Dora and the rest of the nosy CIs know that. His nurse would get no peace until they'd ferreted out the reason for her aversion.

So, trying to protect her as best he could, he said, "First off, let her settle in a bit before you expect her to get into the middle of island life. And, secondly, she's only going to be here for a short time. Why would you think she'd be interested?"

"Oh, I don't know that she will be, but it's always nice to have a fresh face and a new viewpoint in the proceedings. I'm hoping she'll lend a hand once she finds her feet."

Thankfully, before he had to think up another round of excuses as to why Harmony probably wouldn't, Dora and the other ladies were departing with hugs and waves, according to their personal preference.

As he strode down Main Street Cam considered the unlikely friends, each so different and yet all completely devoted to the others. They were the soul and the backbone of the Winter Festival—a point Cam had to concede, despite being almost always annoyed with their attempts to interfere in his life too.

Their organizational skills alone were worth

their collective weight in gold, but along with that they also contributed in so many other ways. Designing and sewing costumes, painting backdrops, deciding on the lighting for the public areas and the decoration of the green, making sure everyone who needed help got it... The list went on and on.

If they'd just accept the fact that Cam wasn't the type to be controlled or tied down, and nor would he be guilt-tripped into things, they'd all get along much better. He'd had enough of that growing up—from his mother. The last thing he needed now was to have four more women fussing over him, trying to get him to do what they thought was best.

When he'd been diagnosed as a type 1 diabetic at the age of four, his mother's reaction had been to coddle him, fearful of what might happen if he did any of the normal childhood activities. If it hadn't been for his grandfather, taking him in hand at the age of eleven and teaching Cam how to control his disease, encouraging him to be more adventurous, Cam had no idea how he might have turned out.

Nearing the cemetery, Cam instinctively

turned in, walking the familiar path to the spot under a gnarled and now bare oak where a number of his ancestors were interred.

"Evening, Grand-Da," he said, reaching down to brush a couple of late-fallen leaves off his grandfather's headstone. "Just left the planning meeting. All the usual nonsense for this time of year. I wonder if there'll ever be a time where things run smoothly."

The bench was cold, yet dry, and the evening breeze brisk, but Cam settled in for a little visit. Stuffing his hands into the pockets of his jacket, he looked up at the sickle moon.

"Got a new temporary nurse in today and I'm hoping she'll work out okay."

He was hoping more than anything else that Harmony Kinkaid wouldn't turn the relatively stable island world upside down.

Wouldn't turn *his* world upside down.

As long as she did her job, he shouldn't care about anything else. He just needed to get through the winter rush with someone he could count on to keep the surgery going and his patients taken care of, along with aiding with any injuries. After that he'd have the time and head space to find a permanent employee.

All he could hope for was a certain level of professionalism and competence from Harmony Kinkaid. If she could produce that, all would be well.

CHAPTER FOUR

DAY THREE OF her island experience and Harmony looked at the clock again, giving a huff. Thank goodness this was a temporary position, because otherwise this place would drive her to drink. She'd been waiting for Dr. MacRurie's next patient to arrive for almost ten minutes and there was no sign of him. No call either.

She'd spent Sunday exploring the surgery, making lists of things she needed to get done. The lower floor held the waiting room, an X-ray room, the records room, two examination rooms and Dr. MacRurie's office, along with a reception/office area for Harmony and, in the back, a kitchenette.

Climbing the steps to the second floor, she'd found a larger office, now clearly used for old records and abandoned furniture, and five bedrooms, which seemed set up to house patients. This had been confirmed when she'd located a relatively modern elevator at the back of the building—big enough to accommodate a stretcher. Having not noticed any corresponding doors downstairs, she'd ridden it down and realized it came out into what she'd assumed to be a maintenance closet behind the kitchenette.

When she'd asked the doctor about the second floor the next morning he'd explained that occasionally they'd have a patient who needed overnight observation. Or, if the weather was forecast to be terrible and he was worried about outlying elderly folks, he'd bring them in and house them there.

While Caitlin had written her up a list of duties, with notations on where to find things, in just that first go-through Harmony had been able to see areas in need of improvement. Caitlin was a fine nurse, as Harmony knew, but her administrative skills left something to be desired. At least in Harmony's opinion.

She'd spent the first part of Monday morning trying to put the records into some semblance of order. The files weren't stored to her preferred specifications, and she had broken a sweat moving armfuls of records back and forth. Then, and only then, had she started on a pile of notes that hadn't been dealt with—probably from the time between when her friend had left and the present.

Luckily she was an expert in interpreting "doctor write," because Cameron MacRurie's penmanship was something to behold. She'd often thought that doctors wrote so poorly because their brains were going faster than their hands could follow. If that were the case, her new employer must be a genius!

They'd opened early, because of the Armistice Day ceremony, and she was down in her office before seven. But her frustration levels had risen as their eight o'clock patient had been a no-show, and the eight thirty had sauntered in almost fifteen minutes late. To add insult to injury, the woman had insisted there was no need for Harmony to do any kind of pre-examination tests.

Not that Harmony hadn't tried to get her job done.

"Dr. MacRurie will expect me to have weighed you, taken your blood pressure and temperature, plus asked you about the reason you're here so I can make notes."

"Och, no," Mrs. Campbell had rebutted, in the strongest Scottish accent Harmony had heard since arriving on Eilean Rurie. And from her steely glare Harmony had been able to tell she meant business too. "The Laird'll do all that himself. I'll show myself in."

And before Harmony had been able to react the elderly lady had marched right past her and into Dr. MacRurie's office without even a knock on the door.

Rushing after her, file in hand, Harmony had expected a reprimand from the doctor, but all he'd said was "Ah, here's your file, Amelia. Thank you, Harmony."

Taking it as a dismissal, and thankful not to have got a flea in her ear from him, she'd scuttled back to her desk. Yet, it had still burned when Mrs. Campbell had marched past her at five past nine without even a fare-thee-well.

She wasn't used to patients totally dismissing her that way, and now, with their nine o'clock also a no-show, she was decidedly out of sorts.

She decided it would be best to ask how she was supposed to handle this type of situation, so she walked down to the doctor's office and knocked.

"Come in," he called, and Harmony pushed

open the door, just in time to see him pulling up his shirt. "Is Mr. Gibson here?"

"Um…no," she replied, surprised to realize he was injecting himself with an insulin pen. Taken off guard, she forgot why she was there and asked, "You're a diabetic?"

"Yes. Have been since I was four."

He said it casually, but Harmony was still taken aback. Caitlin hadn't mentioned this, and all around the room there were pictures of him doing all kinds of dangerous stuff: mountain-climbing, caving, hang gliding, hiking through remote-looking terrain… Not that having diabetes should preclude him from doing any of those things, just as her father's heart condition hadn't stopped him from indulging his own daredevil spirit.

But look how that had ended.

Already in a bit of a snit because of the patients, now she found her mental comparison of Cam to her father was making her cross her arms, trying to hold in the spate of words hovering on her tongue.

Instead of letting them loose, she took a deep breath, then asked, "Did you plan to tell me?"

Cam glanced up, his eyebrows lifted. "Why

would I tell you something so mundane when you'd no doubt find out about it sooner or later?"

Although his tone was even, there was an unusually cool expression in his eyes.

"Well, I'm your nurse. The only other medical practitioner on the island that I know of. What would happen if you went hypo or hyperglycemic and I wasn't aware of your condition?"

"I'm very well versed in the monitoring and treatment of my diabetes, and I haven't had an incident in ages. Don't fuss, Nurse Kinkaid."

She wanted to ask what he meant when he said, "ages," but there was no mistaking the steel in his voice. Not to mention his reversion from calling her Harmony to Nurse Kinkaid, so she kept her mouth shut, for a change.

"Was there something you wanted?"

He was putting away his diabetes kit, and although the chill might have gone from his voice, Harmony still felt the flick of his disapproval keenly.

She adopted a formal tone in return. "What is your official policy on missed appointments?"

"Reschedule the patient."

Really annoyed now, Harmony said, "No, I mean how do I charge them for not showing up nor even calling to say they wouldn't be coming? Do I do it through the mail?"

Cam's eyebrows rose again, and he stared at her for a moment, before chuckling. "Ha! Only do that if you want to have a stream of highly upset people coming in to see you. Don't worry about it."

"But it's a waste of my time, and yours. Don't you charge them at *all*?"

Cam got up and stretched. "Most of the time everyone keeps their appointments, but this time of year things get a little crazy."

Distracted by the sight of his muscles rippling beneath his shirt, Harmony tried to look away, but she had a hard time forcing herself to meet his gaze.

"Since Mr. Gibson hasn't shown up I'm going to run back up to the Manor before the ceremony. After it's over I have a quick house call to make, and then I thought I'd take you around the island and show you where the patients you'll need to visit live. Interested?"

"Sure, that'll be really helpful." She'd been

worried about losing her way on her rounds, so that was a relief.

"Actually, you can come with me to see Mrs. Jacobson too. She's just a few steps away from the surgery, and I'll be asking you to start looking in on her, as well. She's in the final stages of liver failure—cirrhosis caused by hemochromatosis, poor soul. She moved here to be close to her son, Hugh, once she'd decided not to undergo any further treatment. I've had her on a bi-weekly visit, but I think it's time to increase the frequency."

"Do you need me to pull her file?"

"No, I have it here," he replied, tapping the folder on his desk.

He spoke a little more about Mrs. Jacobson's prior treatment, and what he'd prescribed to battle the ascites and hepatic encephalopathy. It was, in effect, palliative care, and Harmony wasn't surprised he wanted to up the number of times she was seen.

"I told Hugh I'd be by at one, so maybe grab something to eat after the ceremony, and if you could be ready at a quarter to, that would be great. Oh, and do you have a pair of wellies?"

She'd been wondering why they needed fifteen minutes to go a few doors down when he asked the question and it distracted her. "I haven't worn Wellington boots since my days in the Guides. Do I need them?"

"Some of the farmyards will be a quagmire after the rain we've had, so they'd be a good idea for when you go to do your rounds."

Unimpressed with the thought of messing up her trainers, which were pretty new and had been a splurge buy, she asked, "Is there somewhere I can buy some?"

Cam shook his head. "You'd have to go to the mainland—or order online and have them delivered, which would take longer. We have a bunch of them up at the Manor. What size do you wear?"

"Seven and a half."

"Okay." He sent her one of his heart-stopping smiles. "I'll hunt out a pair for you."

Cam was already heading for the door and Harmony watched him go, still stinging from his earlier set-down, and annoyed at the way her heart leapt and fluttered whenever he grinned that way.

The thought of spending time with him as he showed her around the island flustered her.

Hopefully it was just because he was her boss and she wasn't used to him yet, she mused, knowing it was more. She was attracted to him—which was another wrinkle in what was already a situation so far outside her comfort zone as to be in a different universe.

It would be a lot easier not to have a physical reaction to him if he were a little less handsome and didn't have a gazillion-kilowatt smile. Not even the knowledge that he was a risk-taking daredevil could stop those butterflies from invading her insides whenever he entered the room or smiled her way.

But it should, she reminded herself. The very last thing she needed was to be attracted to a man like her father. The type of man who put his need for adventure before everything else—even his health, or the people who loved him.

Cam made his escape, wondering how he was going to get through the next month and half.

Harmony Kinkaid, his fussy, big-city nurse administrator, was already making him crazy.

She'd rearranged all his files, so he couldn't find anything. She wanted to come down hard on patients who didn't turn up for their appointments. She'd silently showed her displeasure when he'd mentioned he'd be leaving on a hiking and rock-climbing trip to Peru just after Hogmanay, even when he'd said there'd be a locum to fill in for him.

But it had been her expression when she'd realized he had type 1 diabetes that had really aggravated him. She, of all people, should know it was no reason for him not to live fully.

Thank goodness for Grand-Da, who'd shown Cam that the disease wasn't an impediment to having a good, exciting life.

"It's something to be managed," Grand-Da had told him in his habitual no-nonsense way, that first summer he'd come to stay. "Once you learn how to do that anything is doable. You just have to accept you have it and be smart about it."

Learning how to control the effects of his diabetes had given him a freedom beyond his wildest imagining. Gone had been the days when he'd only watched other boys enjoying themselves, never being allowed to join in. And at the age of thirteen Cam had embraced his new-found independence with gusto. Pitting himself against nature, or against his own limitations or fears, had brought him fully alive.

He'd seen Harmony glance at the pictures on his wall, had almost been able to hear her internal dialog regarding the pastimes he chose. As she was a nurse he was surprised at her reaction. Hell, there were type 1 diabetics playing rough professional sports. It all came down to how you took care of yourself and managed the disease.

Maybe he wouldn't be so testy if it wasn't so close to the opening of the Winter Festival and everyone wasn't going bonkers. He'd had one or other of the CIs on the phone almost constantly, complaining about something or needing help with different situations. They kept trying to get him to recruit Harmony too, but so far he'd been able to still keep them at bay.

Settling into his vehicle, Cam ran his fingers through his hair and sighed.

The truth of it was, for all her annoying qualities, his attraction to Harmony hadn't abated one little bit. All morning, whenever they'd been in the same room, Cam had found himself watching her—not as a boss assessing a new hire's abilities, but as a man admiring a beautiful woman. He'd found himself liking the way she moved, liking the scent—something floral and sweet today—that wafted around her, and her expressions with those flashes of emotion she tried so hard to hide.

And those amazing eyes were golden again today. They had him constantly checking to see whether they'd changed to green again...

Despite her trying to boss him around and compulsively rearranging things, he couldn't get his mind off her.

"Don't be ridiculous," he muttered to himself, as he got True Blue started and, after her usual complaints, into gear. "You only just met her. It's just the draw of the unknown..."

But his words rang hollow in his own ears, and he was still obsessing over Harmony Kinkaid as he drove home, looking forward to spending the rest of the day with her.

And mentally kicking himself because he was.

CHAPTER FIVE

CAM STOOD WITH his head bowed as John Harris read out the list of islanders who'd served in World War I and World War II. The Armistice Day ceremony was being held at the cenotaph at the north end of the village green, and Cam was aware of Harmony standing next to him, all her attention on the elderly wheelchair-bound gentleman.

He was one of the patients she'd be checking on when she was on her rounds, and Cam had promised at least to point out those who were attending, even if he didn't get a chance to introduce her to them all.

As the "Last Post" was played by a cadet, Cam watched in his peripheral vision as Harmony fished a tissue out of her pocket and dabbed at her eyes. He was always moved by the "Last Post" too—the long first call, and the trill of the bugle running and then coming back to the mournful last notes.

John Harris, ninety-eight years old and a veteran of World War II, had tears streaming down his cheeks too, and Cam knew he was probably remembering his old friend Dougal, who'd died the year before. The two men had enlisted together, served together, and had been friends all through their lives.

After two minutes of silence the National Anthem was sung, then the crowd began to disperse and Cam took Harmony over to meet John Harris and his son Martin.

From then on it was a round of introductions, which seemed to last forever, before they could break away and head back to the office.

"Oh, my…" Harmony said, almost as though she were apologizing. "Those ceremonies get to me. My father's family are almost all military, so they always strike home, but I think Grandie would have approved of this one. He liked a nice simple observance rather than a lot of pomp and circumstance."

"I'm glad to hear you think he'd have approved," Cam replied. "Was your father in the military too?"

Her lips pursed as she shook her head. "No. He had a congenital heart defect which made him ineligible. He tried to sign up, to follow in his father's, uncles' and cousins' footsteps, but the army turned him away."

"That must have been hard on him."

Cam wondered why the subject of her father had made those lines come and go between her brows. But they were at the side door of the surgery now, and he opened it so she could step through.

"I guess so," she replied, with a touch of frost in her voice. "But he made up for his disappointment."

Before he could figure out what to say to that, she turned toward the staircase leading to her apartment.

"I'll see you at a quarter to one," she continued. "I promised the CIs I'd meet up with them for lunch and I want to change before you and I go on our tour."

"Don't let them talk you into doing anything you don't want to. The Winter Festival gets crazy, and they've already been trying to get me to recruit you to help. I've been valiantly staving them off."

She paused, her hand on the railing, one foot

on the lower step, and looked back at him over her shoulder. "Why?"

Self-conscious under her golden perusal, he shrugged. "You just didn't seem too keen whenever I mentioned the festival or Christmas."

Her lips twisted briefly to the side, then softened into a rueful little frown. "Sorry," she muttered, and then cleared her throat. "It's not that I don't want to help, it's just... I'm a little low on Christmas spirit this year."

It shouldn't matter to him why. In fact, he should be glad of it, as it meant she'd be disinclined to get too involved, giving him time to get over this unwanted attraction. Yet his curiosity was stronger than any sense of self-preservation. Harmony didn't seem the type to open up very often, so her showing him even a little chink in that practical armor was enticing.

"How come? Just too far from home?"

"That doesn't bother me," she said, but he heard uncertainty in the stout declaration.

Then she sighed, and turned back to face him.

"The truth is my gran died earlier this year, and Christmas was always a special time for us to celebrate together. It just won't be the same without her and Mum."

"Well, you have space here. You could ask your mum to come up and spend the holidays with you."

The cheerful note he'd tried to infuse into his voice seemed to have the opposite effect to what he'd intended as she slowly shook her head.

"Mum's finally getting a life of her own. Her new gentleman friend has invited her to Yorkshire to meet his family, so that's a non-starter." Drawing herself up to her full height and tipping up her chin, she continued, "But it's fine."

That should have been the end of it, but he knew all too well what she was going through—the loneliness that cloaked the soul after the loss of someone pivotal in your life. The feeling that nothing would ever be the same without them, and the unsure sensation of the world being off-kilter, perhaps never to right itself.

"I get it. Really I do," he found himself saying. "Those firsts are always the hardest. When my grand-da died I didn't feel like facing the holidays either."

Harmony's lips came together in what he'd previously thought of as her disapproving expression. But now he was left wondering what it really meant, considering the pain lingering in her eyes.

"You were close to your grandfather?" she asked.

"Oh, yes. Closer to him than to my parents. I lived with him for a couple of years, and I used to come here every holiday I could to be with him. Even when I got older, if it was reading week at university, you name it, I'd be on Eilean Rurie. It was only after I started working with the aid agency that I didn't get back as often as I'd have liked."

"My gran had lived with us since my dad died, when I was six," she replied. Then, as though suddenly aware of what she was saying, she added, "I'm sorry. I don't usually have a pity party in front of my boss. I think the ceremony this morning has made me a little emotional."

"Don't apologize, please. I don't mind."

Those big golden eyes, slightly misty with tears, drew him in…had him fighting not to step forward. She was all he could see. The world had shrunk to just the woman in front of him, so valiantly battling for complete composure.

Normally he shied away from too much emotion, never trusting it to be genuine. His mother had been a master of using feigned sadness or disappointment to manipulate—until she'd realized it no longer worked on him and had turned it off like a tap.

Harmony Kinkaid was just his temporary employee—a woman he'd known for a couple of days. Why, then, was the urge to comfort her so overwhelming?

His heart was suddenly hammering, and alarm bells were going off in his head, but he paid the warning no mind. Instead he stepped closer and rested his hand on her shoulder, rather than on her cheek the way he wanted to. Her lips were soft now, full and inviting.

Begging to be kissed.

Cam exerted a Herculean effort and dragged his gaze away from her mouth to focus once more on her face.

"I'm sorry you won't be with your family this year, and that you've lost someone so important to you that it doesn't even feel worthwhile celebrating, but it'll be okay. You just wait and see."

And his chest grew suddenly tight as tears

gathered at the corners of her eyes again. When the first one slipped free, before he could give in to the urge to wipe it away, she turned and started up the stairs, leaving him staring after her, confusion his only companion.

Cam had been right about the CIs trying to corral Harmony into helping with the festival, but she'd told them she'd only just got to Eilean Rurie and really needed more time to find her feet. While they'd grumbled about it, by the time they'd left the pub Harmony thought they'd given up on the idea.

Crossing the green to the surgery, Harmony thought again about her earlier encounter with Cam. She'd been obsessively going over it, alternately ashamed of telling him anything and grateful for his sympathy. But what totally floored her was her visceral reaction to having him so close.

When he'd touched her shoulder she'd wanted to make the tiny movement that would have been necessary to get close enough to hug him. The simmering attraction she'd felt from the first moment she'd seen him had threatened to boil over. For an instant she'd thought he was going to make the first move…kiss her. She was almost sure his gaze had dropped to her mouth. The anticipation that had fired through her had been like an electric jolt, and just remembering it brought another shock of desire.

"Get a grip, Harmony," she admonished herself out loud, letting herself into the building, her cheeks hot, her insides fluttering as if a wild bird had invaded her stomach. "He was just being kind."

Besides, she hardly knew him. *And* he was her boss. *And* she was off men, to boot.

It was imperative that she got herself together and got real. She was here to do a job and that was all. Not to play Santa Claus, nor to make a fool of herself because she was feeling like Scrooge. And certainly, *definitely*, not to lust after her gorgeous daredevil boss, who had "heartbreaker" written all over him.

The CIs had been quick to tell her that Cam was single, and she'd been thoroughly grilled on her own status. She'd had no problem telling them about her break-up earlier in the year, although not in detail, since it had got them off the subject of Christmas.

She determinedly pushed all thoughts of her

conversation with Cam aside, focusing on work instead. A quick look at the time told her she had just a few minutes to run upstairs and comb her hair before he arrived—if he was on time.

His rather *laissez-faire* attitude toward the way his practice was run would have made her think him a little scatterbrained if he hadn't been so clearly intelligent. But he'd frowned when she'd rearranged the filing system, and given her a blank look when she'd asked why there were over four hundred records when there were less than two hundred and fifty people on the island.

And she was still wondering why they needed fifteen minutes to go just down the road.

He did turn up at the appointed time, and Harmony's heart-rate picked up as she watched him from her bedroom window. He got out of his vehicle to open the gate before driving around to the front of the building. She made herself walk slowly down to join him, neither giving in to nor showing any of the silly eagerness bubbling inside her.

Outside, she found him leaning on the hood of his car, as handsome and relaxed as a magazine model. Clearly he wasn't suffering from the same reaction she had, and she was determined to meet his cool with all the calm in the world.

Cam explained the extra fifteen minutes while they were walking over to the Jacobsons' cottage.

"Hugh is in denial about the terminal aspect of his mother's disease, and he has a tendency to want to speak for her, saying how well she's doing rather than letting her tell me the truth. He's also a bit of a fusspot when it comes to time. If I get there a little early he doesn't have the tea ready yet, so I get a few minutes to talk to Delores alone and find out exactly how she is, and if there are any new developments. I keep the more clinical aspects, like taking her temperature and blood pressure, for when he's in the room, so he feels as though he's in the thick of it."

It made sense, and she made a note of it for future reference. Hearing his logic also made her contemplate how different this job was going to be from her last. There everything had been regulated, and although they'd got the chance to get to know some of their patients quite well, the little personal touches like those

Dr. MacRurie had just described had often been missed.

The visit went as predicted, with Hugh Jacobson greeting them at the door, rushing to the kitchen to make tea, and apologizing for it not being ready when they got there. The doctor winked conspiratorially at Harmony, making her silly stomach flutter, and he pushed open the door to the front room where his patient was.

Mrs. Jacobson was a quiet lady, who smiled when she saw Dr. MacRurie and Harmony and seemed to know the drill. Wasting no time on small-talk, she answered the doctor's questions while her son was out of the room. But then, with a quick glance toward the open door, she grasped Cam's wrist, stopping him midsentence.

"It won't be long now, Cameron," she said, in her soft brogue. "But I just want to make it through Hogmanay. I don't want Hugh to be sad every Christmas because I died around the holiday."

Tears stung the back of Harmony's eyes, but Dr. MacRurie just patted Mrs. Jacobson's shoulder and said, "We'll do our best to see you through till then, Delores."

"Good," she replied, seeming to relax slightly in her chair. "I want to see the lights this year, even if I can't get out to enjoy the festival."

Harmony couldn't tell this sweet lady that it wouldn't matter to her son whether she made it through to the New Year or not. Her passing would hurt him whenever it happened, and he'd miss her every holiday thereafter.

Later, after they'd drunk tea with mother and son and were walking back to the vehicle, Cam said, "She didn't know she had hemochromatosis until after the menopause, and it had already caused extensive liver damage. She's not the complaining type, as you could see, and attributed the symptoms to simply aging. Hopefully we can keep her going the way she wants."

No matter how unprofessional it was, Harmony didn't feel able to discuss it just then. Not when seeing Mrs. Jacobson had brought all the pain of losing her gran rushing to the fore.

She made an noncommittal sound. Then quickly said, "I guess you weren't putting me on when you said there's a Winter Festival, although it's hard to picture." All she saw was a tiny village—nicer today, with the sun out, than it had been the last couple of days, but nothing special.

Cam opened the passenger door of his aged utility vehicle and Harmony tried not to wince at the metallic creak.

As she climbed in, he replied, "Wait and see. I think you'll be pleasantly surprised."

But she was still skeptical. After all, how fancy a show could the inhabitants of a tiny place like this put on?

CHAPTER SIX

CAM WALKED AROUND the front of the vehicle, glancing in at Harmony through the windshield. She was fussing with the seatbelt which, like most things in True Blue didn't work as it should, and just a glimpse of her furrowed brow and pursed lips made him smile.

Cranking open the driver's door, he levered himself into the seat just as she got the belt wrestled into submission. She was casually dressed, but the jeans, white shirt and red anorak did nothing to camouflage her lovely figure. Cam rather wished it did, so he wouldn't find himself admiring it so much.

Firing up the engine, trying to ignore how good Harmony smelled, he dragged his thoughts back to business. "I forgot to ask, can you drive a manual?"

"Yes," she said.

But just as he was coaxing the vehicle into

gear and, and it ground its way into first, he glanced across and saw her concerned expression.

"My grandfather taught me, but although he always said if I could drive a stick shift in Jamaica I could drive anywhere, I don't know if I can manage *this* beast."

Cam chuckled. "No, I have an estate car for you to use. I'm the only one who drives True Blue. She's very persnickety."

"True Blue?"

There was no mistaking the laughter in her voice, and it made Cam's grin widen. "She's held together with baling wire and tape, but she's never let me down anywhere I couldn't walk home."

The sound of her amusement filled the rattling, groaning vehicle and made Cam unaccountably happy. He realized he'd never heard her laugh that way before; not a giggle but full-on belly laughter.

What started as a quick glance at her had him staring, his gaze riveted on her face. Amusement had taken her from beautiful to stunningly gorgeous, and it was only the need to watch where he was driving that tore his attention away.

"You live on a very small island. I'm guessing you'd be able to walk home from just about anywhere—am I right?"

He cleared his throat, being careful not to look at her again. "Yes, but don't tempt fate. We're in this together now."

That exchange seemed to set a good tone for the rest of the time they spent together. Harmony even relaxed slightly, so Cam asked about her grandfather, and heard the story of her grandmother travelling to England alone.

"She explained it by saying that Granddad had 'small pond' syndrome. He wasn't happy with the thought of leaving a place where he was known and had a certain status to start over in a much larger pond, where he'd have to begin again at the bottom."

Cam couldn't really relate. As a child he'd lived in more countries than he had fingers, and before moving back to Eilean Rurie he had seen even more working for the aid agency, which had sent doctors to refugee camps and disaster zones all over the world.

Despite his desire for a stable home when he

was young, if given the chance to start over somewhere new and exciting now, he'd probably take it. With his past experience, being tied to the island sometimes chafed.

Still trying to get a handle on her family, he said, "Oh, I thought at first perhaps it was your father's father who taught you to drive?"

"No," she said. "My dad was half English, half Scottish. No Jamaican roots."

Something in her voice stopped him from asking anything more about her father, so he just said, "How often do you get to go to Jamaica to see your family?"

"I went most summers before I started nursing school. I haven't been back in a while, though, and I should go soon. Granddad isn't getting any younger, and now he's my last grandparent left."

"I hardly knew my mother's parents, and my father's mother died before I was born. I think it made the bond between Grand-Da and me all the stronger."

"Did your mother's parents live far away?"

Cam eased True Blue into neutral and brought her to a stop at a T-junction before he replied. "No. It was my parents who moved around all the time. My dad is an archeologist, my mother's his archivist, and he loves working in the field—the more obscure and distant the dig, the better. The Middle East and Southeast Asia are his specialties."

The peripatetic nature of his childhood was something he rarely, if ever, talked about, and he was glad to be able to divert Harmony.

"Okay, now, it might seem logical to think this road goes all the way around the island, but it doesn't. If you continue along here you get to the Harris farm, and then to a dead end where we have a wind turbine installed. So you need to remember to take the turn here, rather than go straight."

Fighting the wretched gearbox, he made it back into first and turned the corner to continue circling the island. Since he'd introduced her to most of the people she'd be seeing on her rounds, he decided to simply give her the tour and then take her back home.

The less time they spent together, the better.

They crested a slight rise in the rolling terrain and the sea came into sight in the distance.

"Oh! How lovely!" Harmony said suddenly.

"Can we stop for a second? I promised Mum I'd take pictures, and I'd forgotten up until now."

It was a glorious day, although chilly, with a cloudless sky, and he found her reaction to the vista charming. For all his wanderlust, to Cam, Eilean Rurie was the most beautiful place in the world, and he loved to see others appreciate it, as well.

As he brought the vehicle to a halt she fished her phone from her bag and then hopped out. Cam followed, noticing the way the breeze caught her curls and made them bounce.

She started snapping pictures. "I told Mum about the ferry ride, and she asked then if I'd remembered to take any pictures. I felt pretty silly telling her I hadn't."

"Your mum's okay with you being so far away?"

Harmony shrugged lightly. "I don't think she was happy with the idea, but she knew I needed a job, so now she's taking it in her stride, I think. I've been keeping her updated all along the way, and I got a chance to talk to her this morning before her shift. She's sent my other suitcase already, or I'd have asked her to put in a pair of wellies."

"I have a pair for you. At the Manor."

Her lips twitched. They didn't purse, just twitched.

"Did you forget them?"

"No," he said, stuffing his hands in his pockets, not sure whether to be annoyed at her implication. "I washed them off and left them out to dry. We're going to drive right past the front entrance to the Manor anyway, so we'll stop and you can get them."

Her eyes were shining when she turned toward him, and heat radiated up his spine as she smiled.

"Oh! Can I take a look inside? I'm so curious about what it's like."

"Sure," he said, then had to clear his tight throat and get a grip on himself. What was it about her smile that made his entire system go into overdrive? "But we don't start opening up most of the bedrooms until later this week."

Harmony blinked at him, her eyebrows dipping briefly before she turned back to take another picture. He played back his words in his head, trying to figure out her reaction, and then suppressed a groan.

Had he really just mentioned bedrooms, as though they were what she should see? And now that he'd realized the connotations he could picture her in bed—all smooth golden-syrup-and-cinnamon skin and luscious curves, those wild curls spread across his pillow. Somehow, though he didn't know how or why, he knew her eyes would be greener then, inviting him close, and closer yet...

His reaction to the image was visceral: a shock of heat along his spine, lust turning his blood to lava.

She still had her back to him, had made no reply, and he dragged himself from his fantasy to rush into speech, trying to salvage the conversation and his sanity.

"We only keep part of the hotel open for most of the year, since we just get dribs and drabs of visitors. But next week the entire place will be opened up and aired, and the decorating started, so you'll get a chance to see all of it."

"Okay."

That was all she said, leaving him wondering if he'd gotten himself out of the suggestive hole he'd unthinkingly dug.

Harmony took a deep, silent breath, pretending total concentration on her phone, all the while trying to shake her imagined visual of Cam in bed.

Naked.

Aroused.

Making love to her.

Those chiseled lips on hers…his large, capable hands all over her body.

She was blushing. The heat caused by an intense rush of arousal had traveled from her chest into her face. So she kept her back turned to him, trying to get herself under control.

What on earth was wrong with her? She'd met handsome men before, even dated a couple, but none had affected her the way Dr. Cam MacRurie did.

Finally she got herself centered, and although her cheeks still felt warm, she thought she'd dare to turn around.

"I've got enough pictures," she said, trying not to look at him. "Shall we…?"

They got back into the vehicle and he ground it into first.

"True Blue sounds like her gearbox and clutch need some help," she commented, just to break the silence, which was weighing on her and giving her too much time to think.

"We only have a few cars on the island, since a lot of people use bicycles or scooters, so our mechanic went off to look for greener pastures. I'd have to take her over to the mainland on the car ferry to get her looked at. She's sounded like this forever, so I'm not too worried."

They drove through a cut in the low hills—a twisty road, with rough autumn-colored moorland punctuated by the occasional gnarled tree or low copse on each side. In the distance the hills rose, dark stone stark against the heather and grass. It was, Harmony thought, beautiful in a stern, unflinching way.

"Do you get much snow here?"

"Not really—the occasional heavy fall but usually just a light coating. Our location is pretty sheltered, and because the hills aren't very high storms tend to pass over us quickly."

Just then they crested a hill and there below was a small settlement and the sea again beyond. The afternoon light was wonderful, and the sun, which would set about four o'clock, hung low in the sky, casting a golden glow over the whitewashed buildings.

"Our fishing village," Cam said as Harmony leaned forward to see better. "My great-grandfather moved it here after a storm destroyed the old fishing village a little way down the coast. The entire spit of land gave way, and over the years the sea has eaten most of it up. You can still see the old buildings and what remains of the rescue station when the tide is low."

She risked a glance at him, but when heat threatened to overtake her again, looked away.

"How long has your family lived here?" she asked.

"Almost two hundred years," he said, and she couldn't help smiling at his obvious pride. "In 1853 my three-times great-grandfather won the island in a game of whist."

"A game of what?"

"Whist. It's a card game. The story is that the island's owner at the time was a bit of a wastrel. He lost a lot of money to my ancestor, and paid with the land. Charles MacRurie took the island, which was sparsely populated at the

time because it was only used as a summer re-
treat and hunting lodge, and turned it into his
private fiefdom."

"Clearly he wasn't the humble type, since he
named it after himself."

Cam chuckled. "From all accounts he was
not. At all."

They continued around the coast, with Cam
pausing every now and then for her to take pictures, and Harmony keeping the conversation
away from the personal and on the island and
work.

She was amazed to hear there was an alpaca
farm, which produced hand-spun wool, an artists' collective, and a pottery with a world-fa-
mous potter. Somehow it had never occurred
to her that so small a place would have such an
interesting and diverse set of artisans.

When Cam pointed out her patients' homes,
and the side roads she'd need to take to get to
them, she was able to ask informed questions,
since she'd already read all their files. Cam
slanted her a raised-eyebrow glance, but didn't
comment beyond answering her.

As the gates of Rurie Manor came into sight
he said, "The road continues on past Eigg Point,

and then goes back to town, but we'll take the back road when you're finished looking around the Manor."

Call it cowardice, or the effect of the heat she could already feel building in her belly and snaking out to fill her chest, but Harmony had changed her mind.

"Why don't I wait until everything is decorated?" she asked. "I'm due to check on Hillary Carstairs tomorrow, aren't I? So I'll take the car and drive myself back to the surgery. It'll give me a chance to read her file more thoroughly and do any research I need to."

"Sure, if you'd like," Cam replied, giving her a look which she avoided, quite sure her cheeks were red again. "But it wouldn't be a problem for you to come in now."

She firmly refused, even though close up the Manor was so beautiful she itched to get inside and see it for herself.

Instead she put deeds to words, collecting her borrowed Wellingtons and then hightailing it out of Cameron MacRurie's vicinity as fast as possible.

CHAPTER SEVEN

HARMONY WOKE UP to an almighty roar and clatter, which got louder and then seemed to be coming into the surgery itself. They were back to their usual nine o'clock opening schedule, and normally she would have been awake long before seven, but she'd hardly slept and had hit the snooze button a few times.

"What on earth...?"

The noise was coming around the corner of the building, and she could swear that everything in the place, including her teeth, was rattling.

Kneeling on the bed, she pulled back the curtain and saw, in the gray morning light, two large lorries and a caravan going past. As she watched someone jumped out of the first truck to open the gate leading to the Manor and the cavalcade drove through. It was only when the trucks were going up the path that she realized there were a couple of SUVs following behind, as well.

She watched until the last vehicle was through, and the gate was closed behind them, before letting the curtains swing shut again. Reaching over and turning on the bedside lamp, now wide awake, she wondered what was going on. More vehicles than she'd seen on the entire island had just passed her window.

Sliding out of bed, she reached for her bathrobe, resigned to getting an early start on the day, although she'd planned to spend another half an hour in bed. Mum was working afternoons, starting yesterday, so there was no early-morning prework call to look forward to, and no good reason to be up earlier than necessary.

Not that she could talk to her mother about the main thing on her mind—Dr. Cam MacRurie, who'd cost her sleep and had her mind and body in a tailspin. While her mother was no prude, Harmony knew the fact that her daughter seemed to be going ga-ga over a man she'd literally just met wouldn't sit well with Delilah Kinkaid.

Heck, it didn't sit well with Harmony either, but she couldn't get the darn man out of her head.

Tossing and turning half the night, thinking about Cam, had left her frustrated and testy, wishing she could stay in the apartment all day and not have to face him. However, there were tasks that needed to be done in the surgery, and despite Cam telling her there was no rush she preferred to be ahead of the game, rather than stressing when a deadline loomed and she was unprepared.

Having showered and had some oatmeal, she went downstairs to the surgery and was surprised to see, through the front window, a crowd of people on the village green.

Going closer, to look out through the glass, she realized there was more than just people. There were a couple of pieces of what appeared to be farm equipment, some open-back vans, and lots of ladders, loaded pallets, coils of rope and large wooden boxes.

Harmony blinked a few times, trying to figure out if she was seeing things. There were only two hundred and fifty people on the island, give or take, and it appeared that all of them, probably plus a few more, were milling about on the green.

"What are they…?"

She almost had her nose pressed to the glass, trying to see what was happening. In the midst of it all was a figure in a Santa hat she was almost sure was Dora, who was gesticulating this way and that like a conductor on a podium.

Another figure broke from the group and came toward the surgery, and Harmony hurriedly scooted back to her desk.

She'd met the man in the pub—Broderick Thompson—and wasn't sure she liked him very much. He was a smooth talker, a little too full of himself for her liking, and his light gray eyes had seemed to be undressing her rather than holding her gaze.

Hopefully he wasn't on his way to the surgery, but if he was she'd rather present an air of professionalism rather than be caught gawking out of the window.

Sure enough, the door to the entryway opened a few seconds later, and the man who was the gallery owner came in, sleek smile in place, sandy blond hair ruffled by the wind, exposing his scalp.

"Harmony, beautiful lady! I saw the lights come on and came over to ask if you'd be joining us."

"I'm afraid not, Mr. Thompson," she replied, not returning his smile. "I have work to do."

His eyes took a break away from crawling all over her chest to glance around the empty waiting room. When he looked back at her his eyebrows were raised in exaggerated surprise.

"I can see how busy you are. *So* busy that I guess you wouldn't have time for a coffee with me? But I know the surgery doesn't officially open until nine, and Lalli's has opened early for the workers, so I'm sure you can spare a few minutes."

"No, I actually don't have the time."

She made no effort to soften the refusal, and she thought his eyes hardened, although his smile stayed in place. Unfortunately, instead of leaving, as she'd hoped, he actually had the temerity to come over and plunk his skinny bum on the corner of her desk.

"Come on, now. All work and no play makes for a less than *harmonious* life."

Harmony just barely stopped herself from rolling her eyes at his heavy-handed banter. "I really have to get on with my job, Mr. Thompson. Was there anything else you wanted?"

He leaned forward, almost in her space, but Harmony held her ground, clenching her teeth as his gaze dropped to the front of her shirt again.

"Well..."

He let the word trail off suggestively, and Harmony narrowed her eyes. If this twit thought she was going to put up with any of his nonsense let him try her! She was ready.

"Broderick. Not lending a hand outside?"

Cam had come in through the back so quietly neither of them heard him. Harmony jumped with surprise, and when a wave of embarrassed heat rose in her chest she berated herself for it.

She wasn't doing anything wrong.

Broderick Thompson got up and stretched. "Just came in for the First Aid kit. Dora sent me."

Lying creep, Harmony thought, furious enough to want to smack him over the head with the kit once she'd fetched it from the store room. Instead she placed it on the desk, doing her best not to glare.

He picked it up, and gave her another of his smarmy smiles.

"So, what time for coffee later?"

Behind her she heard Cam's office door open, but his footsteps stopped. She knew he was listening, and the thought of him believing she'd go out with Broderick Thompson made her more curt than perhaps she should be.

"I already told you no, Mr. Thompson, and I tried to be polite about it too. If you'd prefer I be rude, ask again."

Broderick's cheeks reddened, but to his credit he just shook his head as he picked up the kit and said, "Can't blame a chap for trying. See you both later."

She restrained the urge to make a rude noise as the door closed behind her, but it was hard not to kiss her teeth. Very aware of Cam, still standing by his door, she reached for the supply list on her desk, intent getting on with the audit she'd put at the top of her day's to-do list. He'd explained that he usually put in a big order for a number of medical necessities just before the festival, in case they were needed, but much of it lasted the rest of the year.

"Whoa," he said, and the amusement in his

voice made her want to blush all over again. "Remind me not to rile you up."

With her nose in the air she swept past him, on her way to the medical stores.

"I think it's be almost inevitable that you will at some point," she retorted, before she could stop herself.

The sound of his laughter smoothed the last of her ruffled feathers and she found herself smiling too as she set to work.

Cam was still chuckling to himself as he sat at his desk to switch on his computer.

Originally he'd come down to see if the noise of the arriving equipment had woken Harmony, and to tell her to take part of the afternoon off since she'd started so early. He truly loved this time of year, despite the stress of putting on the festival, but his excitement had shriveled on finding Broderick Thompson leaning close to Harmony, as though about to kiss her.

Her guilty start when he'd spoken had made the rest of his good humor flee, but hearing her give the other man that set-down had restored it. Clearly she had the good sense to see through that Lothario.

Even though Broderick ran a profitable business at the gallery, somehow acquiring really good artwork and having successful yearly exhibitions, he was a bit of a menace otherwise. The women on the island who had known him longest had learned of his wandering eyes over time, but to him every new arrival was fair game.

Cam wasn't surprised he'd tried it on with Harmony, but her clear and cutting refusal had been a thing of beauty.

Would she do the same to him, should he try to kiss her?

He realized he wanted to—badly. Every movement of her lips, whether they were smiling, pursed, or speaking, made him want to taste them.

And he wanted to know what she'd feel like in his arms. Those amazing curves snuggled against him, her arms around his neck, his mouth on that long, lovely throat.

Or anywhere else on her body she'd let him get at.

Arousal hit him, heating his blood. Shifting in his seat, he tried to banish the vision of a naked Harmony from his mind, so as to not cause himself any more discomfort. For goodness' sakes—what was he? Fifteen? Getting turned on just daydreaming over a woman he hardly knew?

Mind you, Harmony would make any redblooded man think dirty thoughts.

And she made him completely forget what he was supposed to be doing—like actually turning on his computer instead of starting blindly at the still blank screen.

Hitting the switch, he waited for the machine to boot up.

The physical attraction would be so much easier to quell if he didn't actually like her so much. Yes, she was fussy, and bossy, and on a couple of occasions she had reminded him of why he preferred a single life by giving him one of those "oh, really?" glances that activated his stubborn independent streak. But none of that negated his very real desire to get to know her better.

Much better.

Intimately, even.

She was his employee, though. Temporary, but on his payroll nonetheless. Professionalism dictated that he not get involved with her, no matter how short a time she was supposed to be on the island. Besides, there was an innate danger in getting too close to a woman like Harmony, even for a little while. She had the kind of forever vibe he assiduously avoided.

He might be an adrenaline junkie, but forever was one heart-stopping trip he didn't want to go on. Not when it would mean changing the life he enjoyed so much, and having someone else to consider every time he wanted to make a decision.

His childhood, stunted by his mother's fear over his diabetes and his own need to allay her panic, had made him recognize his need to be free of those types of entanglements. Even now, when he was speaking to his mother on the phone, he omitted telling her too much, knowing she'd be frightened to hear about his adventures. That was about enough of an emotional burden as he could manage.

The computer beeped, the cursor flashed, waiting for him to put in his password. Doing so absently, Cam found himself remembering Harmony's sadness when she'd spoken about how much she missed her grandmother.

He understood, completely. The first Christmas after Grand-Da died had been the hardest of Cam's life. Only the fellowship of the islanders, who missed the old man as much as Cam did, had eased the pain. It was a shame Harmony and her mother wouldn't be together to remember the old lady and all the good times the three had shared.

Then he frowned as the first notification to pop up on his screen was an email from Dora entitled To-Do List.

"Really?" he muttered to himself. "Don't you think that after four years I know what needs to be done?"

Yet still he opened it, and sat running through the various points until the phone rang.

Since Harmony was in the back, he called out, "I've got it!" and picked up the receiver.

"Cam MacRurie speaking."

"Cam? Are you coming by today?"

"Hello, Hillary," he said, noting the strain in the woman's voice. "Is everything all right?"

"Oh, yes, of course. I just wondered…"

"My new nurse, Harmony, is scheduled to come out and see you, Hill," he said gently. "Will that be okay with you?"

"Oh, yes, of course," she replied, and the automatic answer told him more than her words. "It's just that I don't *know* her. How will I know it's her? And I haven't had a chance to tidy up…"

"Don't worry about it, Hill. I'll come out with her and introduce her properly. That way next time you'll know who it is. Will that suit?"

"I… I…"

She faltered, and Cam waited, guessing she was trying to gather her thoughts.

"So you'll come, then?"

"Yes, Hill. I will." He infused as much of a soothing tone into his voice as he could. "I'll see you in a little while."

"Thank you." The relief in her voice was patent. "Thank you, Cam."

After he'd hung up the phone, Harmony, who'd come to the door, asked, "Her anxiety getting the best of her?"

Cam nodded, pleased that she'd picked up on that from the file. Hillary Carstairs had been born with spina bifida, yet had lived life to the fullest, getting around with leg braces and a cane until her later years. She had two children, one of whom still lived at home and helped his father on the farm.

Now confined to a wheelchair, Hill had developed agoraphobia and an anxiety disorder, which made her increasingly isolated. He'd prescribed antianxiety medication, which she'd refused to take, and offered to refer her to a specialist, but again she'd refused—perhaps because of having to go to the mainland for appointments.

It was at times like this when Cam felt the restrictive nature of the island keenly, and chafed at not being able to provide what was necessary.

"I'll ride out with you," he said to Harmony. "It'll allay some of her stress, and hopefully she'll be okay with you coming alone the next time."

"Okay, but it seems a shame to interrupt your day that way. No doubt you have scads of stuff to do."

Cam happily closed the email from Dora and grinned. "It's not an issue. Hill's health is the most important."

Besides, Hillary and Gavin's farm was in one of his favorite parts of the island, and showing it to Harmony suddenly seemed like a great idea. In fact, there was nothing he'd like more—although why that was wasn't something he wanted to think about too deeply.

CHAPTER EIGHT

THE CARSTAIRS' FARMHOUSE was filled with the evidence of Hillary's weaving business, although Harmony had seen no sign of the alpacas when they drove up, which was disappointing.

Hillary Carstairs was stressed and apologetic, but Harmony was adept at handling patients with anxiety disorders, and had her calmed down in a fairly short time. Hillary even agreed to allow Harmony to do her examination and change her catheter.

"Everything looks good," Harmony told the older lady as she helped her back into her wheelchair. "But I see from your chart that you've refused treatment for your anxiety disorder and agoraphobia. May I ask why?"

Hillary's eyes shifted away and she knotted her fingers together. For a moment Harmony thought she didn't intend to answer. When she finally spoke there was an air of surrender in the words.

"I've been poked and prodded and I've taken medication my entire life. Why would I add even more? Besides, going anywhere in this contraption takes so much effort. It's not fair to Gav."

Harmony tweaked the ends of Hillary's skirt so it lay flat, thinking through her answer before saying, "You realize what an anomaly you are, right?"

Hillary frowned slightly. "What do you mean?"

"Well, you've lived to be in your sixties with spina bifida. Had two children and a full life. It's only in the last few decades that spina bifida has been considered something other than a childhood disorder, since people diagnosed with it weren't expected to live very long. Why give up now?"

Hillary shrugged, but she was obviously listening, her gaze steady on Harmony's face, so she continued speaking.

"You already have some limitations placed on you by your disorder. Why not deal with what you can, so you can continue enjoying your life to its fullest?"

There was no reply, but as Harmony packed up her kit she left it at that, hoping she'd given her patient some food for thought.

They left the bedroom and found Cam and Gavin, Hillary's husband, in the large farmhouse kitchen, leaning on the counter, sipping from teacups.

Gavin was a short, stocky redhead with an infectious grin, who asked, "All right, then, love?"

"Yes," Hillary said, smiling back at him. "Everything is fine."

But Harmony found herself the recipient of a piercing interrogatory glance from Gavin, who only visibly relaxed when Harmony nodded her agreement.

"Good, good… Want a cup of tea, ladies?"

At their affirmative responses he set about pouring cups for them from the pot, while a black-and-white collie came over to say hello to Harmony. She bent to pet it, getting a lovely cold nose in her neck and a couple of licks before the dog slunk off in typical collie style to flop down on a cushion in front of the fireplace.

Gavin said, "I was just telling Cam that I've moved the flock up to the old croft, which is why they weren't hanging over the fence watching to see who was arriving."

"They're a nosy lot," Hillary said. "I miss seeing them when I look out the window."

"I was hoping to get a glimpse of them when we arrived," Harmony said, adding a murmur of thanks as she took the cup from Gavin.

"Cam can take you up to get a look," he replied, turning to Cam as he continued. "Take the four-wheeler."

"I will," said Cam.

"Oh, that's not necessary," Harmony said, at the same time.

Cam laughed. "I think it's a grand idea. And, if you don't mind, I'd like to show her Ada Tor."

"Go right ahead," Gavin replied, resting his hand on his wife's shoulder as he passed. "I don't need the UTV again until later this evening."

Everyone else looked pleased as punch at this idea, and Harmony realized she'd look churlish and ungrateful by refusing, so she plastered a smile on her face. But she wondered what kind of vehicle it was they'd be taking, what kind of terrain they'd be traversing, and if any of this was safe.

She got her answer after they'd finished their tea. While she stowed her bag in True Blue, Cam and Gavin went into the barn. After a short time there was the clatter of an engine, which sounded like a large lawn mower, and a small four-wheeled vehicle came stuttering out. It had two seats, a flatbed in the back, no doors, and it bumped across the farmyard as though it had a complete lack of shocks.

Filled with trepidation, she cautiously approached as Cam brought it to a halt nearby.

At least it probably couldn't go very fast, she thought as she got in.

But with the way Cam drove it over the rutted tracks it might as well have been a race car. Even terrified half out of her wits, and hanging on for dear life, Harmony had to admit he handled the little vehicle well, with the kind of casual capability she couldn't help but admire.

When they got to a gate she got out rather shakily to open it, and then closed it behind the UTV once he'd driven it through.

"All right, there?" he asked with a grin as she got back in, before setting off again after her curt nod.

The land undulated, but Harmony got the

sense they were going more uphill than down—
a supposition that was proved as they went
around a rise and she looked back to see the
farmhouse below them. Ahead in the distance
was a stone building, and even farther away
what looked like a jumble of boulders all piled
up together.

At the sound of the UTV, the alpacas came
moseying out, and Harmony couldn't stop her
little squeak of pleasure on seeing their cute,
curious faces. Cam brought the vehicle to a halt
and Harmony got out for a closer look.

The alpacas kept their distance, with the one
in the front eyeing her suspiciously. As she got
closer to the fence it huffed, and she stopped.

Cam came up beside her and pointed. "That's
Sandro—the male. He's pretty protective of his
flock. Not much of a spitter, according to Gav,
but I wouldn't chance going much closer when
his ears are flat like that."

"I was hoping to pet one," Harmony replied.
"They look so soft…"

"Got their winter coats on," he replied, and
she saw him looking at her out of the corner of
her eye. "You really like animals, don't you?"

"I do. Gran had a little scruffy dog for years,

and he and I were best buds. She didn't want to get another after Hobo died, and I was so busy I didn't think I'd have enough time to care for an animal myself, but recently I've really been thinking about getting a pet soon." It was her turn to look at him, now, wanting to see what his expression told her as she asked, "Don't you like animals?"

"Love them," he said, which came as no surprise to her, really. He seemed the type.

"So how come you don't have a dog or three?"

Cam shook his head. "Maybe one day I will, but right now a pet would tie me down too much. Every time I want to go away I'd have to find someone to look after it."

Unable to decide whether that was a smart or a selfish way to be, Harmony made no comment. Instead she made soft, hopefully enticing sounds to the alpacas, trying to coax them closer, but they weren't interested and, after a short time, they turned and started back toward the building.

"That was where Gavin's parents lived," Cam said. "He and his four siblings were born and grew up in that crofter's cottage. Gav built the farmhouse for himself and Hillary when they married, and after his parents had passed away, and none of the children wanted to come back here to live, he converted it into a supplementary barn."

"Wow. Seven people in that little building? Must have been cramped," he said as they were heading back to the vehicle.

"I think they were used to it," he said, as they got back in. "And they spent enough time outdoors to make it doable. They all had to help on the farm when they weren't at school, and with sheep—which is all Gav's father had back then—there's always something needs doing."

Further conversation was curtailed by the racket of the motor starting up. Then they were off again, heading for the up-thrust of boulders, which she discovered was far larger and higher than she'd first thought.

Cam left the path and bumped across the field, straight for it. Harmony was hanging on, wanting to tell him to slow down but finding the words caught in her throat. He finally slowed, then stopped within a couple of yards of the rocks. When he turned off the vehicle the sudden silence rang in her ears.

There was a wild, stark beauty to the landscape: gray rocks interspersed with autumn-colored ground cover and a few bare-limbed trees. In the sky a raptor of some type circled, and the whisper of the wind was the only sound. When Cam spoke it was in a low tone, as though he didn't want to break the spell of quietude.

"Come on. Let me show you the best view in all Eilean Rurie."

They got out, and Harmony followed Cam to the boulders. But when he started to climb she hung back, shaking her head.

"I'm not going up there," she said, trying not to show her instinctive fear. "I don't know how to climb."

Looking back at her, he said, "This isn't climbing, really. Just a little scramble. It's perfectly safe, and if you're not feeling confident go ahead of me and I'll guide you."

Oh, how she regretted not wearing the Wellington boots, which would have given her a solid reason not even to attempt the climb. But she'd worn her trainers instead, and with Cam's eager expression and outstretched hand she was completely torn.

Anything to do with climbing—even what

he called a scramble up some boulders—filled her with terror.

"Scared?" he asked, his eyebrows going up. "Are you afraid of heights?"

Was there a condescending note in his question? Whether there was or wasn't, it got Harmony's dander up and she lifted her chin.

"No, I'm not," she said, gathering her courage and stepping up on the first rock. "Lead the way."

Cam climbed with the ease of familiarity, but made sure to look back often and make sure Harmony wasn't having any difficulties.

They didn't talk, except when he warned her of a longer step, or a spot where there was a crack to watch out for. She was obviously inexperienced, hesitating in places, searching for a good hand or foothold in areas where, to him, it was obvious. But he had to admit she was game, and she grew even higher in his estimation.

He'd been sure she'd refuse to go to the top of Ada Tor. In fact, he would swear she'd been petrified when he'd suggested it. Yet here she was, more than halfway to the top, soldiering on. Hard not to admire her grit.

When he got to the top he reached back to help her up the last little bit, but she ignored his hand and scrambled up by herself. As she stood beside him, dusting her hands off on her jeans, he watched her look around, and he saw the dawning pleasure on her face at the vista laid out before her.

The land fell away in dips and swirls, the contours and colors reminding him of a Van Gogh painting, and in the distance lay the sea, a smooth blue expanse so far away. Just visible to the southeast were the roofs of the town, and to the west the little crescent of buildings making up the fishing village. Sheep and a few horses dotted the fields, but it was the quality of the air and the perfect height of the sun that really brought out the island's splendor.

"How lovely…" she breathed, turning to look back toward where the mainland was just a smudge on the horizon above the trees along the northern coast.

"I told you it was the best view," he said, and found himself taking in the familiar sight and appreciating it even more than usual. Something in her awestruck expression made him see it through fresh eyes.

"Is this rock formation natural?" she asked, still turning slowly to see everything all over again.

"I think it is," he replied. "Although there isn't another like it on the island. Legend has it that there's a Celtic princess buried under it, but I don't think it's true."

"Hence the name Ada Tor?"

"Yes."

He sat down on a handy rock, still gazing out. After a moment she joined him, and he shuffled over to give her more room. Her fresh, sweet scent wafted over him and stirred something deep inside.

In the distance a truck rumbled along the road, and she pointed to it briefly. "I can't get used to seeing so many vehicles here all of a sudden. It's surprising after hardly seeing any at all."

"They're probably delivering Christmas trees to Angus's farm. He always gets his early because he has so much work to do. The rest will come later in the week."

Harmony sighed quietly, and he somehow

knew she was thinking of her family and all she'd miss this year.

"Will you tell me what you used to do with your gran and your mum for Christmas? I'm curious to know about some of your customs."

She gave him a sideways glance, before staring out at where the truck had disappeared into a dip in the land.

"It wasn't much different from other English families, I guess," she said, but then proceeded to prove herself wrong.

It was as if a dam had broken, and Cam could only listen as she listed all the things she'd be missing this year. There were things he'd never heard of—what on earth was a gizzada, or jonkanoo?—but other things he completely understood. Lots of poinsettias, since they were such a popular tradition in the Caribbean. Watching favorite movies, listening to beloved songs. Decorating the tree together and inviting everyone they knew to come by to exchange gifts and have drinks.

It wasn't so different from what happened here, he thought as she fell silent. Some different cultural traditions, of course, but the picture she painted of family and friends, of a community sharing laughter and joy, labor and company, was the same.

Without thought he looped his arm around her shoulders and gave her a quick squeeze. When she stiffened he almost let his arm drop, but then she turned her face to look at him and he froze, captivated and enticed by her solemn eyes, her soft lips.

The wind had died, and their faces were so close together her breath rushed warm across his mouth. Cam inhaled, wanting to take it into his lungs, hold on to it just for a moment.

Want spiked through his veins, so strong it wrapped around his chest, making it tight. It was there in her eyes too, he thought, the same anticipation and curiosity that was heating him through.

Then she blinked, color flooding her cheeks with a rose-toned blush, and Cam finally heeded the danger signs flashing in his head as they pulled away simultaneously.

The sensation of having her warm, soft body against his side lingered, though, reminding him of what was so close and yet should be ignored.

He cleared his throat, searching for a memory of what they'd been talking about so as to bring them back from the sensual ledge they'd stepped out on. "Christmas at your house sounds wonderful. I'm sorry you won't have that this year."

She turned her face away from his, but not before he saw that her eyes were misty.

"I just have to accept it'll never be that way again," she said quietly, a little quaver in her voice. Abruptly she rose and turned back toward where they'd climbed up. "Let's get down now. I have work to do."

He followed her lead without comment, but inside he was wondering what, if anything he could do to make the season ahead better for her.

Despite knowing it was ridiculous, his heart had ached on hearing her pour out her pain. And he certainly shouldn't want to hold her, comfort her, kiss her the way he was drawn to do.

Yet that was exactly how he felt.

CHAPTER NINE

I'VE HAD ENOUGH of this...

"This" was the Christmas music playing through the office, and Cameron MacRurie's occasional attempts to sing along.

He might be Laird of Eilean Rurie, and a good, well-respected doctor, but his singing left a lot to be desired!

Yet even as she had the sour thought Harmony found herself smiling and shaking her head. The song playing was an old one, sung by a crooner her grandmother had loved.

Harmony could almost hear Gran saying, *Lawd, tell the man to stop caterwauling.* But it would have been said through laughter, and the old lady would have gone and sung with him, trying desperately to get him in tune.

Not that it would have helped Cam, who was clearly tone deaf.

As the days had gone by she'd found herself

shaking her head at Cam's behavior a lot—when she wasn't ready to murder him, that was.

On the day after they'd climbed Ada Tor, while still reeling from their near-kiss, she had been horrified to see him up on the half-built scaffolding being put up around one of the oaks on the green. Then, the next day, she'd come into the surgery to find not only that Cam had beaten her to work for a change, but that the reception area was packed to the rafters with boxes, as well.

"What on earth is all this?"

It had taken everything inside her to keep her voice below a shriek—especially when she'd spied the cobwebs liberally festooning the cartons.

"Decorations," he'd said, with just a hint of smugness in his voice. "I checked the calendar and, since we don't have any patients today, I figured it was the perfect time to bring them down. Don't look so annoyed."

Annoyed? She'd been livid.

But then he'd added, "It's a part of being Laird. I have to set a good example. And I hope, as my employee, you'll see fit to help me."

So she'd been stuck. How could she have refused without looking as truculent as she'd felt?

The kicker was she'd enjoyed it—once she'd gotten over her snit. Even being hyperaware of his movements, of every accidental touch of their fingers or his body brushing past hers, she'd found herself relaxing into the joy of bringing Christmas to the surgery.

The decorations were a mixed bag: some obviously old, some new, some elegant, others as chintzy as they came. But Cam had a story for almost all of them.

It had taken them most of the day to get most of them set up, with a break for lunch at Sanjit's restaurant. Cam's grandmother's porcelain Christmas village, dating from the fifties, delicately beautiful, had been placed on a shelf where it could be admired out of reach of little hands. His grand-da's collection of Christmas greetings cards from around the world had been strung on lengths of tinsel along one wall. An impressive nutcracker collection had ended up liberally covering almost every surface possible in the surgery, and paper festoons were hung all over the ceiling, with old-fashioned lanterns in between.

They'd argued over the placement of those, with Cam wanting to put them up willy-nilly and Harmony insisting on a more regulated design. She'd won, of course, and he'd been forced to admit that it looked better than he'd have ever imagined.

"The Christmas trees are coming in a couple of days by ferry," he'd told her, when she'd asked what he wanted to do with the tree ornaments. "We'll get that done up once I pick one out."

Spending that time with him had been so much fun, but in a strange way seeing him like that, being in close proximity with him again for an entire day, had also felt dangerous. Both the trip to the Carstairs' farm and their working together to decorate had taken him out of the "hunky doctor fantasy material" zone into something more intimate.

She kept replaying that moment she'd thought he would kiss her in her mind, telling herself she wouldn't have let it happen, but knowing she would have given in to her own desire. To her own chagrin she wanted to experience his kisses—and more.

That evening, curled up in front of the fireplace, Harmony had realized just how much she was starting to *like* Cam on top of being physically attracted to him. She liked his enthusiasm. The way he wasn't afraid to go head to head with her, but how he also backed down once he realized she just might be right. His tenderness as he'd brought out his grandparents' favorite decorations and told her their stories had touched something deep inside her.

Her ex, Logan, was the ultimate pragmatist. The kind of serious man who thought everything through and then announced the way things would go. He wasn't sentimental in the slightest, and he'd shied away from anything that even remotely resembled emotion even when they were alone. She'd thought him safe and steady, only to have him prove otherwise.

Somehow she was sure everything would be different with a man like Cameron MacRurie. It was there in his eyes. In the way he listened so intently when she was talking. In his smile… in his speech…even in the way he moved. The kind of man he was called out to the secret self she alone knew: the romantic, sensual side of her she rarely acknowledged.

And that secret part of herself wanted Cam—badly.

But, she reminded herself, Cam was a daredevil, a risk taker and, like her father, he appeared to turn a blind eye to a medical condition that could cause serious damage if not managed properly. Worse, it could be deadly.

As a nurse she knew she was being unreasonable about Cam's diabetes. With all the new ways of treating and managing type 1, people with the disease were living fuller lives than ever before.

However, as a woman, and one who knew what it was like to lose someone because they refused to accept their limitations, Cam was the last kind of man she needed in her life. Getting close to people just led to heartbreak, in her opinion.

Meeting him had had her thinking of her father more often than she usually did, drawing comparisons that made her both angry and sad. And no doubt having just lost Gran contributed to her general train of thought.

As the December first opening of the Winter Festival fast approached, the entire island was like a beehive, with everyone buzzing to get everything in place. Vendors were starting to arrive, and Harmony had been surprised at the number of people suddenly on the island, all pitching in.

Not even the rain, which came hard and fast one afternoon, deterred the workers for long.

"Come on, come on!"

The CIs took refuge in the surgery as the thunderstorm rolled overhead, and Dora was not pleased at the delay.

"Telling the storm to hurry won't make it pass any faster," Katherine commented helpfully, and then took a sip of her tea. "Besides, for once we're ahead of schedule. Relax for a moment."

"Hush!" Ingrid interjected, as herself, Dora, and Sela all gave the other woman dirty looks. "You'll jinx us."

Just then Cam came in, his hair soaked, his shirt damp enough to cling to his chest and arms. Harmony hurriedly looked away, his delectability quotient making her mouth water. Rising, she to the back and got him a towel, just as one of the CIs asked what on earth he'd been doing to get so wet.

"Got caught with just my windbreaker on,"

he said, taking the towel and giving Harmony a smile that almost melted her on the spot. "Gave my hooded anorak to one of the lads from the mainland who didn't have one. I have another at home."

Another reason to like him—although there were so many others screaming at her to keep her distance.

"I'm glad you're here, ladies. There's something I want to discuss with you."

Harmony wasn't sure whether he was including her or not, but Cam didn't tell her to come with the others when they trooped into his office, so she stayed where she was, feeling ridiculously put out.

It wasn't as though she was *involved* in the preparations for the festival. In fact, other than the surgery decor she'd done her level best to stay out of it. Although watching it all happen around her had made her realize what a Scrooge she was being. Everyone else, from the oldest to the youngest, was lending a hand, and excited about it too.

Even her shut-ins wanted to hear every detail of what was happening in the village. Mr. Harris, in particular, had been talking her ear off about how things had been done "in the old Laird's time."

"All this hullabaloo about scaffolding around the trees to hang the lights? Not in our day! We'd shinny up those trees like squirrels and string the lights that way."

"Now, Da," his son Martin had said, sending Harmony a wry smile. "You have to admit the trees were smaller back then."

"Och, not so much smaller. And there was that big old oak that came down in the storm of seventy-two. She was a grand old tree—taller than any of them left there now!"

"Will you come to see all the lights, Mr. Harris?"

Harmony had just finished doing the older man's wellness check, noting that his oxygen saturation levels were fairly good and the edema in his feet was reduced. He'd been diagnosed with level two congestive heart failure just over a year ago, but had continued to work on the family farm until he'd fallen one day while out looking for lambs. After that, his son had put his foot down—although, he admitted, keeping his father in was like herding cats.

Cam had told her that Martin had gotten a gaggle of geese and put his father in charge of those, to make sure he had something to do that was close to the house.

"Of course." He'd sounded outraged that she'd suggested otherwise. "Wouldn't be Christmas without seeing the fair and all the lights and the gewgaws people put up, would it?"

Harmony was brought back to the present when she heard Dora clearly through the closed office door.

"It's not possible, Cam. Not at this late stage."

Then came a babble of voices, and a few shushing sounds, all of which left Harmony eaten up with curiosity. So much so that she was tempted to put her ear to the door—an impulse she was ashamed of immediately thereafter.

"'Eavesdroppers hear no good of themselves,'" she muttered, once more quoting her Gran, who'd been full of annoying sayings.

Oh, great, this place is turning me into my grandmother.

Thankfully, just then the door opened, giving her something else to concentrate on.

"Hello, miss," said a Christmas tree with legs,

coming into the surgery. "Just dropping this off for the Laird. I'll leave it here, by the door, if that's okay with you?"

"Yes, that should be fine," she said, eyeing the huge fir as the man carrying it finally extricated himself from its grasp.

The ceilings in the surgery were high, but she wondered if it would fit or if, like in a Christmas comedy, they'd have to cut a hole up to the second floor to accommodate it. Trust Cam to choose the biggest tree of them all!

The CIs came out of Cam's office like a tornado, with Dora in the center. She was scowling, but Harmony thought the twinkle in her eyes looked rather dangerously amused.

"Good—the rain's stopped. Back at it, ladies. Especially since the Laird has added to our plate. Harmony, I'll see you over at the Manor this evening, right?"

Surprised, Harmony was about to say she didn't know what Dora was talking about when Cam quickly replied, "Yes, she'll be there."

Then the CIs were off, already bickering again.

"What's going on at the Manor tonight?"

"Progress meeting and the Manor's tree-decorating and lighting. I like for everyone to have a hand in it and see all the decorations before the craziness starts in earnest," he said, heading for the surgery Christmas tree. He whistled. "She's a beauty, isn't she? Not as magnificent as the Manor tree, of course, but perfect for in here."

"Don't you think it's a bit big? And when did you plan to tell me about tonight?"

Cam was rummaging in a box and emerged, triumphant, with the tree stand before he replied, "It's the perfect size—and I thought the CIs would have told you, so I didn't bother."

He shrugged apologetically.

Did he have to look so adorable doing that? she wondered, inexplicably annoyed.

They spent the rest of the afternoon putting up the tree—which was only just short enough for the star to fit at the top. It took both of them to wrestle the tree into the stand, and then Harmony went to get water to fill the receptacle while Cam cut away the netting holding the boughs against the trunk.

"Don't put the water in yet," he said, pulling the tree a little farther from the wall. "We're going to have to decorate the side that'll be seen through the window and then push it over. The water will make it heavier and harder to move."

They argued over the lights.

"If you wrap some close to the trunk, and then more at the edges, you'll get better depth of light," she said.

"*Depth of light?* What on earth does that mean?" he asked, his lips quirking.

"I can't believe you're the Laird of the North Pole of Scotland and don't understand that most basic of concepts."

He rolled his eyes, but gave in eventually. Of course then they argued about whether the white lights or the colored should go near the trunk, but she gave in on that one and they put the colored ones inside and white outside.

As they took out ornaments and placed them on the tree they looked specifically for those related to the Winter Festival theme of "love."

Finding a tattered but beautiful little heart made of felt, with an intricate design embroidered in the center, Harmony held it up. "This is perfect. A little stained, but right in line with the theme."

"Wow," Cam said, holding out his hand for her to give it to him. "I haven't seen this in years. The design is like a luckenbooth—a traditional Scottish betrothal gift. My grandmother made it, and Grand-Da used to put it on the tree in the Manor. I wonder how it got in with these?"

Instead of putting it on the tree, Cam slipped it into his pocket and Harmony's chest ached, just a little, when she noticed him touching the spot where he'd secreted it every now and again.

Later, after they'd finished decorating the tree and tidying up, he said he was going back to the Manor. When, a few minutes later, she saw him crossing the green, she knew he was going to the churchyard, as he so often did, to visit with his grandfather.

Why that should make her like him even more—*want* him even more—she didn't dare consider.

CHAPTER TEN

"WELL, GRAND-DA, EVERYTHING seems to be going smoothly, for a change. The trees are strung, the shops and roadways are decorated, and the firs all came in without incident. Remember that one year when they didn't get loaded onto the ferry?"

Cam had the churchyard to himself, as he usually did, but he was stooping at his grandfather's headstone since he'd forgotten to bring anything to wipe off the bench. It wasn't unusual for him to come by and give Grand-Da updates on his life, but today was different. He'd started with the mundane because the specific felt too hard.

"Tonight is Manor night. The place looks beautiful, as always. Got a really nice tree this year. I think you'd be pleased."

Despite his inviting her a few more times since his *faux pas*, Harmony still hadn't been up to the Manor. In a way he was glad, since she'd be seeing it at its best tonight. On the other hand he was nervous. He wanted her to like it, even love it, the way he always had.

Running his finger over his grandfather's name, Cam forced himself to get to the point.

Grand-Da had always hated prevarication.

Get to the point, son.

Cam could hear his grand-da's voice in his head, the tone a mixture of annoyance and amusement. He'd always been able to talk to the old man about anything, although sometimes it had taken a while for it to come out, since Cam had been used to keeping his own counsel about a lot of things.

"I…" He cleared his throat and tried again. "Harmony found the heart. The one Gran made for you the first Christmas you were together. I don't know how it got into the boxes in the surgery, or why I never noticed it was missing."

It made him remember the story Grand-Da had told, about meeting Gran in London, knowing right away that he wanted to marry her. Gran hadn't been interested. She'd had other plans.

She was a city girl, your Gran. Had no interest in a Scottish country lad—doctor or no.

Oh, she gave me a merry chase, and I had to seduce her around to my way of thinking, but I knew there would never be another like her in my life. If she hadn't eventually had me I'd be a lonely old man now. Instead I always have her love to keep me company.

It was as though he was sitting in front of the fire again with Grand-Da, chuckling to himself over the story. He'd been too young then to appreciate the strength and depths of true love. Yet the tale had always touched him, deep inside, and now to suddenly have it come back…

"Are you trying to tell me something, Grand-Da?" he asked aloud.

Cam was a man of science, but there were times like this when he had to wonder about greater forces and how they could manifest in life.

He didn't *want* to want Harmony. Didn't believe real love could blossom in the space of less than three weeks. Yet the draw she exerted, the mix of comfort and excitement he felt in her presence, was unprecedented in his experience. And when he'd seen that heart in her hand, that gorgeous, beaming smile, her eyes alight with pleasure, something had shifted inside him. A sea change of the soul.

"She's my employee, Grand-Da, and she's bossy. Plus, she's not at all into adventuring. I think it scares her."

The first was a sticking point, but the second he really didn't mind. In fact, he rather liked arguing with Harmony. She was logical, and forthright, and didn't hesitate to give as good as she got—which made it all fun.

The third point, however, was a bad one.

His friend Josh had sent him a video of a group BASE jumping with wingsuits. One of the men had been wearing a helmet cam and the footage as they arrowed along the side of the mountain was amazing. Josh had suggested they learn, and make it a part of their next adventure trip, and Cam had been researching equipment and locations when Harmony had come in to ask him a question.

She'd taken one look at the video playing on his computer and had frozen, her lips tightening, those lines between her brows suddenly appearing.

"Looks like fun, doesn't it?" he'd asked.

"No."

It had come out so forcefully, it had taken him aback.

"It looks like craziness. The type of stupidity that can get people killed."

Then she'd turned and walked out, apparently forgetting what it was she'd come for, or so disturbed she hadn't been able to bear to stay in the room.

"She's not for me, Grand-Da. I won't be hemmed in by anyone again. I need someone who'll want to go on adventures with me—not nag me to take care of myself, or get bent out of shape every time I want to do something fun."

It was just the wind rustling through the branches, but it sounded suspiciously like Grand-Da's laugh.

"Right—enough of this," Cam said, levering to his feet. "I'll just put it all out of my mind, get through the festival and send her on her way again."

It felt good to have made the decision, but he found he'd taken the heart out of his pocket, was holding it in the palm of his hand.

For a moment he thought about leaving the heart on Grand-Da's headstone, but instead he put it gently back into the pocket of his coat.

He'd never known his grandmother, who'd died the year he was born, but suddenly he felt closer to her, handling something she'd made. A piece of her heart in the form of a heart.

Touching Grand-Da's stone one more time, he went over to Grandma's and touched it too.

And when he left the churchyard he felt both at peace and more confused than when he got there.

"First time at the Manor?" Dora asked Harmony as they stood to one side in the Manor's ballroom, each juggling a little plate of hors d'oeuvres and a drink.

"That obvious? I'm gawping, aren't I?"

And who could blame her? Everything about the house made her want to gasp. It might have been converted to a hotel, but it had lost none of its charm or its grandeur. For goodness' sakes, it had a real, live ballroom, complete with intricate parquet flooring, plaster swags on the walls and ceilings, and massive gold mirrors, which reflected the bank of windows on the other side of the room.

"I think we all did the first time we got a

chance to see inside the manor," Katherine replied. "It's a thing of beauty."

Harmony couldn't argue with that assessment. She'd had an Elizabeth-Bennett-sees-Pemberley moment the first time she'd glimpsed Rurie Manor, but she'd have never imagined how truly glorious the inside of the old house would be.

"When Cam told me most of it was a hotel I pictured them having gutted the place to modernize it and make it usable, but they've really kept all the lovely old features and atmosphere, haven't they?"

"Oh, yes," Sela agreed. "The Manor has been lucky in her custodians. The MacRurie family has kept it wonderfully. And in this day and age that's no small feat."

"The family has always been smart about it," Ingrid said, gesturing with a piece of celery for emphasis. "I think it was Cam's great-grandfather who turned it into a corporation and a trust, so they could avoid a lot of death duties and keep the place running. Not that they were lacking in funds. They all have that entrepreneurial and inventive streak in them, so they weren't dependent on inheritances alone."

"Really?" This was another facet of Cam's family coming to light for Harmony, and she couldn't hide her curiosity.

Dora nodded, swallowing a bite of cake before elaborating. "Cam's however many times great-grandfather—the first one to come here—was a train baron, who had a number of patents for various parts and equipment the railroads used. And the old Laird—Cam's grandfather—invented some kind of... What was it, girls?"

"A valve," Katherine supplied.

"Yes—a valve for a nebulizer machine to make it work better. And Cam's got a few patents himself...for safety equipment, I believe."

"He needs it," Harmony said, hearing the snap in her own voice and regretting it the moment she'd spoken.

Dora gave her a bump with her hip—Harmony assumed because she didn't have a hand free to swat her with.

"He's adventurous—but that's a good thing in a man, isn't it? Who wants an old fuddy-duddy?"

Harmony would have argued the point, except the topic of their conversation chose that moment to come over to where they were standing.

"Everyone having a good time?" he asked, with one of those smiles that never failed to make Harmony's knees weak. "Had enough to eat? Put an ornament or three on the tree?"

"I don't think that poor tree can take even one more bit of decorating, Cam. Especially the spot where the children were standing."

His smile turned to a grin. "Yeah, that side's looking a little heavy low down, but they had a grand time doing it."

"Have you taken Harmony on the tour yet?" Dora asked—a little too innocently to Harmony's ears.

"No, I thought I'd wait until things calm down a bit. I have to make my rounds and keep things flowing."

"You don't have to—"

What should have been a polite declining of the tour earned her another hip-bump from Dora and a poke in the back from Katherine to boot.

"What?" she asked, since what they'd done was obvious. "Cam's been running around like a chicken with its head cut off. He doesn't need to give me a tour if he doesn't want to."

Cam rolled his eyes. "Just keep her here until

things quiet down and I'll be back to get her," he said to the CIs, adding, "Don't let her slip away. You know she'll probably try."

"Back at you," Sela muttered behind Harmony's back.

And before Harmony could ask the other woman what, exactly, she meant by that, the CIs started arguing about the configuration of the vendors' caravans parked in the field behind the green and the moment was lost.

Every time she tried to give the CIs the slip and get out of there before the end of the party she was foiled. She didn't know why she was so resistant to getting a tour of the house from Cam. Okay, that was a lie. She didn't want to be alone with him right now. Not after seeing him so carefully putting that felt heart into his pocket, with a hint of deeply held emotion that had just melted her heart.

Gorgeous Cam in a wetsuit could be used as fantasy fodder. Dr. Cam could be treated strictly as an employer. Daredevil Cam could be firmly held at bay. But tender Cam? Sentimental Cam, who had immediately gone off to speak to his grand-da after she'd found that little ornament?

That Cam might well be irresistible, and Harmony knew her limitations.

But he wouldn't take no for an answer. As the staff were cleaning up, and the CIs were saying their goodbyes, he firmly guided her back into the hotel and took her through it completely. Even the kitchens, and upstairs to see the guest bedrooms.

Everywhere was beautifully decorated for the holidays, and lit in such a way as to enhance the best features of the house and its ornamentation.

"Rurie Manor is beautiful, Cam. Even the kitchens."

He laughed softly, taking her elbow to lead her back to the staircase. Just that small touch had heat pooling low in her belly. His obvious love of the house his ancestors had lived in and cared for all those years was patent, and she liked him even more for it. There was no hint of him taking it for granted, or being in any way anything but appreciative of being able to live there and oversee its upkeep.

"My ancestors loved Victorian splendor— even the later ones—so whenever there were renovations or updates to be done they naturally leaned in that direction. I'm not complaining, though. They really tried their hardest to keep the best features of the house."

"They did a wonderful job—and I can see you're carrying on the tradition."

At the foot of the grand staircase he hesitated. From farther down the hall she could hear staff talking softly, the clink of crockery and glassware, and the sound of a trolley being wheeled across the floor. There was the front door, just a matter of feet away, and Harmony knew she should make her departure. But she didn't.

The warmth of his hand on her arm, the fresh, warm scent of him, the way his gaze traced her face, all conspired to keep her there.

"Would you like to see my little corner of the Manor?"

No smile on his face. His voice low and serious.

Harmony's world tilted, leaving her unsteady, frightened, and she knew that a decision lay before her like the drop off a cliff.

Walk away and stay safe or step over?

Would she fly or plummet?

"I don't know that I should," she said, being honest, hearing the anxiety she was fighting echoing in her voice. Or was it the rush of desire through her veins making it quiver that way?

Cam's fingers shifted on her arm and he stepped a little closer. Without thought she moved to meet him, so they were only a hand span apart.

"It probably wouldn't be wise," he agreed, even as his head dipped toward her and her lips rose in invitation.

The kiss was light at first, an exploration, but it went to Harmony's head like a shot of one hundred percent proof rum. Firm lips searched hers, drawing her closer, setting her alight with a wild surge of arousal. Her arms went around his neck instinctively, and his encircled her waist, pulling her flush against his chest. The sound he made low in his throat washed through her—a benediction and a promise, all wrapped into one.

Deepening the kiss felt inevitable. Right and true to what was growing inside her. But the force of it almost knocked her off her feet. Clinging to him, she surrendered to the fire, taking his scent into her lungs with each rushed inhalation, her body tightening and softening all at once.

When he broke the kiss, lifted his head, she kept her eyes closed a little longer, savoring the untamable zing of passion discovered as it thrummed beneath her skin.

Finally forcing open lids that felt weighed down with need, she found herself trapped in his gaze, and the gleam of his desire, the rapt, stark lines of his face, let her know she wasn't alone in the wanting.

Then common sense crashed the party. And although she wished with all her heart she could just show it to the door, she knew she wouldn't.

Cam must have seen it on her face, because he sighed gently and brushed a finger over her cheek.

"Did you drive?" he asked.

"No," she replied, regretfully sliding her arms down from around his neck. Although her hands didn't seem to want to let him go, coming to rest on his broad chest. The feel of his racing heart beneath her fingertips almost made her change her mind about going.

"I'll walk you down," he said.

"Okay."

She couldn't help hoping he might kiss her goodnight. And he did better than that, kissing her silly in the apartment foyer, just inside the door.

Harmony lost herself in his arms. Every sipping kiss, each deeper exploration of her mouth, each brush of his hands, which had somehow found their way under her coat, dragging her under.

"You're delicious," he said into her neck, his voice muffled by the fur collar of her coat. "I should go before I can't."

"Yes, you should," she agreed, dragging his mouth back to hers, aware of the dichotomy of her words and actions.

She didn't want him to go. That much was obvious. But how much further was she willing to take this?

Letting him go, taking a step back, was the hardest thing she'd ever done, but somehow she achieved it.

"This is *so* not a good idea." She swallowed, trying to sound normal when every nerve in her body was tingling, her libido gone haywire. "You're my boss."

Cam's eyes were dark, his pupils so dilated

they looked black, and when he scrubbed his fingers through his hair she saw his frustration.

Then one corner of his mouth kicked up. "Your temporary boss."

A huff of amusement escaped her throat, although there was nothing laughable about the situation. "True, but…"

She wanted to say she wasn't into casual sex, and that he wasn't the kind of man she'd ever get involved with otherwise. Wanted to list the complications their sleeping together might cause to a working relationship. Probably point out that there was no way they could sneak around without the entire island knowing what was happening.

Yet none of it crossed her lips. Mainly because it didn't seem terribly important just then.

"Look," he said, holding up both hands as though in surrender. "I know neither of us planned on this happening, but I'm not averse to us…*enjoying* each other while you're here."

Harmony thought about what he'd said. The temporary nature of it should be a turn-off, but strangely it wasn't.

Cam MacRurie wasn't the kind of man she'd ever get seriously involved with. He was too much like her father—a reckless adventure-seeker, who didn't take his medical condition seriously enough. She might have been young when her father died, but she remembered the turmoil, the pain both her mum and herself had gone through. It had shattered their world, left them devastated and emotionally scarred.

No, she realized. If she was going to be able to enjoy whatever this was sparking electricity between them, it would have to be with the inner understanding of the relationship's transient nature. Once she embraced that she'd be okay, because then she wouldn't get emotionally involved.

And, man, did she want to enjoy Cam. He was a temptation she hadn't expected and didn't want to resist. Her entire body reacted to the thought, and in that instant her mind was made up.

Slipping past him, she started up the stairs, and when he didn't follow she turned her head to look at him over her shoulder.

"Aren't you coming up?"

CHAPTER ELEVEN

HE KNEW HE shouldn't go up to her apartment. Despite what he'd said to her, Cam knew he was probably already in over his head. Making love to Harmony might just drown him. But in the back of his mind his grand-da's words rang.

Being afraid is never a good reason not to do something, son. It's a reason to consider whatever you're about to do carefully, but not a good reason to avoid trying.

Harmony frightened him badly. The way he felt when he was with her, worse when he held her in his arms, was beyond any sensation he'd ever known. It made him want to run, to avoid going deeper, and yet she was irresistible.

So he followed her gently swaying hips up the stairs, his arousal climbing with each step he took, anticipation sparking along his spine as he watched her slip off her coat.

Earlier that evening he'd noticed how her red sweater gave her skin a beautiful glow, had thought it was the perfect color for her. Now all he wanted was to get rid of it, so as to get to the golden skin beneath.

The lure of the unknown was heady.

What kind of lover would she be?

The need to know was like a fire in his soul, a kind of insanity he couldn't wait to embrace.

She was fitting the key into the door when he came up behind her on the landing. He couldn't keep his hands off her, and encircled her waist from the back, nuzzling her hair aside to set his lips on her neck.

Harmony shivered, a little moan breaking in her throat. Encouraged, he kissed and licked, scraping his teeth gently over the frantic pulse. When her head fell back against his shoulder, giving him better access, Cam took full advantage.

Then she had the door open and they shuffled into the hallway, his arms still around her, his mouth still on her skin.

"Cam…"

God, the breathiness in her voice almost undid him. He turned her in his arms, ravenous for her mouth again. The urgency he was fighting seemed matched by her own. Tugging and pulling, breaking away from each other's mouths only long enough to get her sweater off over her head, they were soon stripped to the waist.

He picked her up, and she wrapped her legs around his hips as he carried her through the darkness to her bed. They tumbled onto it, locked together, as though fused by passion.

Now—now he could explore that luscious body the way he'd wanted to the very first time he set eyes on her.

He took his time, despite his driving need, slowly removing the rest of her clothes, touching, kissing, caressing each inch of her body as he did so. She did the same to him, rolling him onto his back and straddling his thighs to get at his fly.

There was a moment of shared laughter as they realized he still had his boots on and, now they were trapped in his trousers, he couldn't reach them. She levered them off, then removed his socks. Tugging off his trousers, she began a slow rise up along his legs, teasing him the way he'd teased her.

After a very short time Cam sat up to yank her against his chest.

"Why'd you stop me?" she asked.

But he knew she knew why, because she was making him crazy, and he told her so, receiving another long, passionate kiss in response.

Lying side by side, they discovered each other's weak spots, the places and touches that made the breath catch, the body tremble, that had moans and soft cries of pleasure filling the room.

Their passion built, but Cam wouldn't be rushed, and when she tried to hurry him along he captured her roving, unrelenting hands and held them above her head.

"Behave."

It was a hoarse rumble, and the sound she made in response made his body tighten even more.

"I don't think that's really what you want, is it?" she replied, twisting her wrists between his fingers and arching her back so her breasts rubbed back and forth against his chest.

"No," he admitted. "But I want to take my time, to make it good for you, Harmony."

She froze, and in the dim light filtering through the curtain he saw her eyes close for a moment.

When they opened she'd quieted, and she said, "Kiss me again, Cam."

He'd never been happier to comply with a request in his life.

Sinking into the sensation of mouth on mouth, the sweet tangle of her tongue with his, was as natural as inhaling. When he released her wrists and her hands found his body again—gentler now, not as insistent—the sweep of them across his skin set his nerve endings afire.

Coming up for breath, he didn't know whether minutes or hours had passed—knew only that the desire he'd thought so intense before had grown exponentially, become impossible to contain.

Rolling to the side of the bed, he searched along the ground with his hands. Harmony snuggled up to his back, wrapping a leg over his, her lips weaving magic spells along his nape and across his shoulders.

She paused long enough to ask, "What are you doing?"

"Trying to find my trousers. I have a condom in my wallet."

"Mmm..." She was back at her sorcery, shifting behind him, her mouth following the line of his spine, her hand fluttering over his stomach and heading south.

With a harsh sound of triumph he found his clothes, dragged them toward him. Fumbling for his wallet, he had to pause to grab her hand, lest she make him lose control.

She giggled and he rolled over, trapping her beneath his body. "You're a bad, bad girl."

Harmony blinked up at him. "And you like it, don't you?"

No need to answer. She knew he more than liked it.

Keeping her still as best he could, he fished out the condom.

"Want me to put it on?" she asked.

"Oh, hell, no. That would finish me off."

She laughed softly again, and replied, "No finishing without me."

He couldn't help laughing with her as he rolled away to put on the condom—and she was waiting, arms outstretched, when he rolled back.

"Are you sure you're ready?" he asked. The need to make it perfect for her was paramount in his mind.

"Come here" was her only reply, and she

suited actions to words, drawing him close, welcoming him into her body.

And of course he obeyed, finally where he'd dreamt of being since the day Harmony Kinkaid had landed on Eilean Rurie.

In her bed and in her arms.

Harmony awoke the morning after the Manor party alone. Cam had left before daylight, and although she hadn't wanted him to go, she knew her time on the island would be far more complicated if he didn't. People tended to look askance at women who slept with their bosses.

Not that it worried her overly much. December was a stone's throw away, the festival set to begin. By the end of January she'd be gone, and whatever gossip and ill feelings they might inspire with their affair would die down quickly once she left. She was more than willing to deal with the fallout for a couple of months if she could keep seeing Cam.

The night had been amazing. Magical, in a way. At least for her. Who knew that laughter could add such a new dimension to sex? Logan had been as businesslike in bed as he was in every other facet of life.

Funny to know that she'd felt closer to Cam, more connected, than she ever had with a man she'd spent two years with. It came from knowing Cam MacRurie cared—actually cared about her experience rather than just his own.

When Logan had dropped his bombshell she'd been more angry than hurt, which had made her question her motives for being with him to begin with. It had become comfortable, and his staid demeanor had seemed to make him the perfect partner. Yet, in the end his defection hadn't broken her heart as much as dented her pride.

Being with Cam seemed risky—way outside her comfort zone in a million ways—but since it was preordained to last only for a short time, she could simply enjoy his company without too much angst.

Checking the time, she hopped out of bed and into the shower, smiling to herself at a few unusually achy muscles, all an indication of how thoroughly loved she'd been the night before.

Her phone rang right on time, and Harmony hurried to pick it up.

"Hi, Mum. Everything all right?"

"Yes, yes," her mum replied, as she always did.

Sometimes Harmony wondered what her mother wasn't sharing, perhaps in an effort not to distress her daughter.

"You sound bright and cheerful this morning."

Harmony stifled the chuckle rising in her throat. "It's a beautiful day here, and last night there was a party up at the Manor. I had a good time."

"Hmm..." Her mother didn't sound convinced. "Are things still crazy there with the festival? No chance of you coming to Yorkshire over the holidays? Even for a couple of days?"

"No, Mum." Why did her mother keep trying to rope her into her Yorkshire trip? "I'll have to be here for the duration. There's supposed to be hundreds of people coming through, and although Cam says there'll be additional medical help on hand, he and I will still be the first line of defense."

"Okay, okay. It's just..."

There was a wistful tone to her mum's voice... a sorrow Harmony felt down to her toes.

"It's just what, Mum?"

"Oh, nothing important. Tell me more about what's going on there."

Lowering herself to the edge of the bed, Harmony said, "No, Mum. Tell me what's making you sad. I'm not a baby anymore, who needs to be protected. I want to know."

There was a long silence, and when her mum spoke next Harmony knew she was near tears, if not already crying.

"It's just that I miss you…and the closer it gets to Christmas, the harder it gets."

"Oh, Mum. I miss you too. But you have your trip to look forward to, and Fred to keep you company…"

"But it's not the same. I was dreading Christmas, and I didn't feel up to any of the things we used to do, but now…"

How could she have been so blinded by her own grief and hurt as not to realize that her mum probably didn't know how to face the holidays without Gran? After all, she'd felt the same way when her mum had said she wouldn't be at home for Christmas, but she hadn't had the brains to make the connection then.

Harmony's heart hurt, and tears were filling her eyes to slip down her face. But she knew she had to be strong for her mother—just as her mum had been strong for her all these years.

"Listen, Mum. I know you miss Gran, but she wouldn't want you be wallowing in grief. I can almost hear her saying, *Lawks, who turned on de tap?* if she knew you were crying over her."

It made her mum laugh through her tears, the way Harmony had known it would, to hear Harmony impersonate her grandmother.

"I know nothing is the same this year," she continued gently. "But maybe it's time for you to think about *you*, to figure out what's best for you rather than anyone else. Start a new tradition…teach Fred how to bake a Christmas cake. I don't have the answers, and I'm so sorry I'm not there for you when you need me, but I love you and I want you to be okay."

"Thank you, love," her mum said, after a little pause and what sounded like a blowing of her nose. "You're right, you know. Even if you'd been here it still wouldn't have been the same, and we might have ended up moping around instead of enjoying any of it. And haven't I always been the one telling you to go off and live your own life? But here I am…crying because you've done just that."

"This job is only temporary, Mum." Why did this reminder to her mother make her suddenly feel even more depressed? "I'll be back before you can convert my room into whatever you've been planning all these years."

That earned her a heartier chuckle than her mum had been able to manage before, and they finished their conversation on a lighter note than when it had started.

But Harmony's heart was still heavy as she finished getting ready and headed off downstairs to open up the clinic. Although, the secretive intimate smile Cam gave her when he came in a few minutes later did a lot to lift her mood.

Though the smile on his face faded, concern darkening his eyes. "What's wrong?" he asked, his gaze searching hers.

She didn't know why, but it made her smile. "Don't worry, it's not remorse over a wild night."

He visibly relaxed, coming over to perch on the edge of her desk, lifting a gentle finger to touch her cheek. "Wild, huh? Not sure how to take that. But don't change the subject. You've been crying."

How on earth did he know that, when she'd

been careful to use an extra touch of concealer under her eyes to camouflage the signs?

"I was talking to my mum and I realized what an insensitive beast I've been."

He was so easy to talk to, with his eyes never leaving hers, all his concentration on what she was saying as it all poured out of her.

"How could I not realize how much harder it would be for *her*, this first Christmas without Gran?" she concluded, trying her best not to let the tears start up again.

"You're dealing with your own grief," he said, his hand on her shoulder providing more comfort than a simple touch should. "It's made it hard to see that her grief is what made her agree to go to Yorkshire with Fred. All you saw was her abandoning you, and the loss of all the things that meant Christmas to you."

"You're right," she agreed, miserable again.

"Harmony, come into my office and away from the windows. I think you need a hug, and if I give you one here then I may as well have slept all night in that wonderful bed of yours."

She chuckled, but got up, wanting that hug in the worst way.

"Wonderful, was it?" she teased, as she followed him into the office and watched him close the door behind them.

"Or wild, if you prefer," he retorted, enveloping her in his arms, taking her weight as she leaned against him.

At once she was more relaxed, and muscles she hadn't even realized were tight unraveled in the warmth of his embrace.

"Either one works for me," she mumbled, wishing they could go upstairs and do a hands-on assessment of which adjective worked better.

If she wasn't careful, she warned herself, Cam would turn her into a sex addict, and the withdrawal symptoms when she left would be horrendous.

CHAPTER TWELVE

"HARMONY, YOU HAVE to help me!"

Hearing Dora's near shout on the other end of the line made Harmony's heart-rate go into overdrive.

"What's wrong? Are you hurt? Where are you?"

"I'm at home. Come quickly."

"Do you need Cam?"

He was out, checking on a visitor who'd fallen off his scooter earlier in the afternoon, leaving Harmony to close up the clinic. She hoped she could deal with whatever it was happening to Dora.

"No, no. Just you. Hurry!"

Grabbing her jacket and a medical kit from the back, Harmony swiftly locked up the surgery. Normally in an emergency she'd drive, although Dora's house was only a short way away, but with the number of people on the roads, and walking all over the place, it would be a lot quicker to walk.

Or in this case trot—which was what she did, weaving her way through the throngs of visitors.

Hard to believe it was already midway through December, with the Winter Festival in full swing. Harder yet for Harmony to reconcile the sleepy little village she'd first seen on arrival with the wonderland it had become.

The lights, banners, decorations, and Christmas trees in every window gave the village a truly festive air. And it wasn't just the village. A night drive around the island revealed light-encrusted fences, trees, and houses, a variety of seasonal lawn decor, and even a forest of firs in a field, all lit up and open to the public to walk through.

"Angus Stewart does that every year," Cam had told her. "He tried growing a grove of firs, but the soil was wrong, so instead he buys the trees and sets them up like a miniature forest. And right in the center he has baskets of rowan and a stack of Cailleach logs for anyone who wants burn them in his nightly bonfire."

"Cailleach logs?" she'd asked, bewildered. "What are those? And why burn the rowan?"

"Cailleach is also known as the Hag of Winter. It's an old tradition to carve her face on a log and then burn it to banish the cold, the darkness, and any coming hardship. The rowan is supposed to burn away any hard feelings between friends or family members."

Every day she learned something new. When she'd first heard about the festival she'd pictured something far less elaborate—although, to be fair, Cam *had* tried to warn her from the beginning.

On the other side of the green the fair grounds were a mass of people all day, and up until it closed at ten at night. She'd been twice already—once with the CIs and again with Cam—and she'd likened it to a cross between a Renaissance fair and a long, ongoing party. While she'd politely passed on the haggis, she'd enjoyed the Yule bread and the clootie pudding.

"It similar to a Jamaican Christmas pudding," she'd told the CIs. "But blander. Ours has rum, and a lot more fruit. My gran kept her fruit soaking in rum and wine all year long, so as to have it ready for Christmas."

The CIs had exchanged strange looks over that tidbit, but Harmony hadn't been able to get them to say why. Maybe it sounded alien to them—just as things like the Cailleach and neeps and nips did to her. It was a whole different world, but she was loving it.

Especially since Cam, as the Laird, had lately taken to wearing a kilt.

It was easy now to see why women went bonkers over men in kilts. With his calves on full display, and the green, red and gold tartan swinging when he walked, he looked delicious!

Finally getting to Dora's cottage, she raced up the path to knock on the door. It was flung open, and a frazzled-looking Dora dragged her inside.

"Thank goodness you're here."

She hadn't released Harmony's arm, just continued to pull her through the living area toward the kitchen, her cat meowing and weaving between their legs. Meanwhile, Harmony was trying to assess whether Dora had an injury anywhere. With her strange behavior, maybe she'd fallen and hit her head?

"I need help."

"With what? Are you hurt?"

They got to the kitchen and Dora pointed inside, the picture of tragedy personified.

"Mince pies!"

"Can you imagine?" Harmony said later that night to Cam, when he arrived at her apartment. "There I am, thinking she's hurt, running like an idiot down the street to her place, only to find out she's baking mince pies and has fallen behind on production! I could have strangled her."

Her expression of outrage had Cam too busy laughing to reply, and Harmony flung a cushion at him in response, even though she was laughing too.

"She had me there until nine o'clock, cranking out twenty dozen pies. Thank goodness that's one of the things Mum makes, so I wasn't completely clueless. It could have been clootie pudding."

Cam didn't mention that twenty dozen was the number of pies Dora usually made every evening by herself during the festival.

"Did you have a good time, despite being used as unpaid labor?" he asked.

"Oh, I got paid," she replied, with a groan, flopping back onto the couch.

The royal blue terrycloth robe she was wearing gaped slightly at the throat, giving him a tantalizing glimpse of cleavage.

"I ate enough mince pies to give myself colic, but, yes, I enjoyed it thoroughly. Dora makes me laugh."

Her eyes glowed, amber tonight, and her smiling face warmed him quicker than the roaring fire. He went over and poked the logs, suddenly wishing she was up at the Manor with him.

They'd agreed for discretion's sake that he'd come down to see her at night when he could, since she'd either have to drive up to the Manor or he'd have to walk her home. Both of those scenarios would make it clear to anyone seeing them what was going on.

Each night since that first one he'd told himself it would be good to take a break, to sleep in his own bed and not get too used to having her in his arms. And each evening after dinner, when he was sure the island was settling down for the night, he'd found himself at the surgery side door, letting himself in.

She'd become his new obsession—and he

was beginning to think she was far more dangerous than skydiving, caving and free-diving all rolled into one.

"I think the cat's out of the bag for us," he said, not wanting to spook her, but being honest. He didn't want anyone to make a comment she wasn't prepared for.

"I thought it might be," she replied, a cautious note in her voice. "You coming out of the surgery the other night instead of driving down from the Manor was probably more than enough to set tongues wagging."

Most visitors to the island came fully prepared to enjoy the sights and were a good-humored lot. There had only been one skirmish so far, when a pair of friends, having had too much beer, had got into a wrestling match outside the pub. It had been swiftly broken up, and the two friends had been sheepish after their nonsense, and apologetic.

But when the call had gone out for Cam to come and examine the patient, who was sitting on the curb outside The Ladies from Hades, he'd been with Harmony, and had had to leave from there right away to investigate.

He had to ask. "Do you mind? That people know we're seeing each other?"

What was he going to do if she said yes and decided they should stop?

"Do you?"

He still had his back to her, facing the fireplace, but he stuck the poker back into its stand and turned around.

"No." Not only didn't he mind, but he didn't care either. "It's really no one's business but ours."

"Okay."

"What does that mean, Harmony? That you do mind but you're okay with it?"

Her smile was beatific, a balm to his racing heart.

"No, I don't mind. We're adults having a good time with each other. Sure, the employer/ employee aspect might make people a little upset, but I don't think they'll tar and feather me."

The muscles in Cam's neck relaxed.

But then she added, "Besides, I won't be here that much longer. It'll all blow over after I'm gone."

The words struck him like a claymore to the

gut. It was the one thing he didn't want to think about—had assiduously avoided contemplating.

"Have you started looking at applicants yet?"

She sounded so cool, as though discussing the weather, while his insides rebelled at the notion of her leaving. Somehow, though, he had to match her calm. He, who more than everyone knew her leaving was both inevitable and right, wouldn't be the one to quibble.

"It'll have to be when things wind down, I'm afraid. There's just no time for it now."

"Fair enough," she said, rolling her shoulders against the arm of the couch, dropping her gaze for a second before meeting his again.

Her eyes had changed—gone from amber to green.

"Do you know your eyes change color?"

She tilted her head as though unsurprised. "I've been told that."

Cam stalked closer to the sofa, those amazing eyes following his every step. "Sometimes they're gold, sometimes hazel, and now they're green."

"It's the genetics wheel of fortune," she replied. "My dad's family mostly have green eyes, and my mum's father came from near a place called Seaford Town, where there's a settlement founded by Germans who immigrated to Jamaica. His eyes are light too, so I got the recessive genes."

Beside her now, Cam sank down onto the couch, and she moved over to give him space to fit right into the inward curve of her waist. He braced one hand on the back of the couch, the other on the arm, bracketing her, hemming her in.

She didn't move, just watched him.

"Doesn't explain why they change color like that."

"Does it matter?"

She touched his face, a butterfly brush of soft fingers, soothing and arousing all at once.

It did to him. Was it an emotional barometer he could use to interpret her mood? Or just a trick of the light? A reflection of the color she was wearing?

"You're beautiful," he heard himself say, the spur-of-the-moment words flowing off his tongue.

Harmony smiled—a seductive curve of her lips that drew him to them—and Cam had no intention of resisting. All this talk about her leaving made him mad, ravenous for her, as though putting his mark on that glorious body, making her cry out with pleasure, would somehow make her stay.

But he held back. Once he started kissing Harmony it was hard to stop. He wanted to make her a little crazy, and watch her while she came apart.

He snaked a hand under her robe, found the soft flesh of her thigh. "What do you have on under here?"

The touch of her tongue to the middle of her lower lip sent heat up his spine, had his body tightening with need.

"Why don't you look and see?"

Using his free hand, he tugged on the tie at her waist—just as his phone rang.

Cam dropped his chin to his chest and cursed.

Harmony laughed. "Such language, Dr. MacRurie. You should be ashamed."

He moved over to pick up the phone from the hall table, still muttering invectives under his breath. "Cam MacRurie."

"Cam, it's Gillian. Those guests I was telling you about are at it again. The mother has tripped near the bonfire and got a nasty burn on her leg. Can you come take a look?"

Suppressing another curse, Cam replied, "I'm on my way," before hanging up.

"What's going on?" Harmony had sat up and tightened the belt on her robe again—damn it.

"The couple staying over at Gillian Strom's are up to their old tricks. Mother has got burned by the bonfire."

They'd already gotten drunk one night and had a nasty argument in front of all the other guests, and their kids—one eleven and the other thirteen—were menaces. Cam was just about ready to send them packing.

"Need me to go with you?"

Sighing, he pulled his coat off the rack and shook his head. "No, stay where it's warm. Depending on what I find when I get there I might have to head straight back to the Manor."

He'd have to walk up to get True Blue and, depending on how late he was, coming back down to the surgery might not be feasible.

"Just take the estate car and your emergency bag from the surgery. Then come back when you're finished." She shrugged, seeming unconcerned, but those lines came and went between her eyes. "We already agreed our secret is probably out. Would it matter terribly if we're completely out in the open about what's going on?"

"If I had time I'd come over there and kiss you for saying that." Cam was shrugging on his coat, bracing himself for the stiff breeze he knew was awaiting him outside. "Keys?"

"On the hook by the door," she replied, getting up. "And in case you were still wondering…"

When she opened her robe Cam froze, every sinew straining to go back to her. She was completely nude, her skin glowing with a natural golden-brown light that seemed to come from within. Her lush body, all soft curves and secret glorious places he loved to explore, was the epitome of everything he desired, all in plain sight.

"Just to maybe give you an incentive to come back," she said, a little smile coming and going across her face.

"I'll be as quick as I can," he choked out.

He forced himself to turn toward the door.

Wanting nothing more than to stay.

CHAPTER THIRTEEN

A STORM ROLLED through the following day, bringing a coating of snow that, to Harmony's mind, added the final touch to the Winter Festival scene. To her surprise, she was enjoying the season far more than she'd expected or even wanted to—probably because everyone seemed so determined to make her a part of things. On one hand, it was heartwarming. On the other, she sometimes viewed it as almost a betrayal of Mum and Gran, although she knew neither of them would want her feeling that way.

"Don't get attached," Katherine warned her as she stopped by the clinic in the early afternoon to drop off a package for Cam. "Snow never lasts long around here. Something to do with the sea currents and how fast the storms pass over."

Harmony was more intrigued by the package than the Eilean Rurie weather patterns.

"What's in here, Katherine? It smells divine."

The older woman shrugged and said, "I don't know. Just dropping it off for Dora. Probably something for up at the Manor."

Giving the package an appreciative sniff, Harmony got up to take it into Cam's office. "Darn it," she said. "I hope I can get him to share. It smells a lot like one of my gran's gizzadas."

"Your gran's what?"

"Gizzada. It's a little tart with coconut filling." Harmony paused in Cam's doorway to look back at Katherine. "I've been such a slug this year. If I'd thought of it I'd have ordered the ingredients and made some for you all."

"Well, too late now, I should think," Katherine said in her brisk way. "Unless you want desiccated coconut. There's always some of that around."

"No, that wouldn't work. You need real coconut—straight from the shell and grated."

"Good luck finding that anywhere around here," Katherine called. "I have to run. Make sure Cam gets that, please."

"Yes, ma'am," Harmony muttered to the sound of the closing door.

Katherine, of all the CIs, was the hardest to

get to know. Both Sela and Ingrid had asked for her help during the Winter Festival, giving her an opportunity to get better acquainted with them. Katherine, however, seemed to be a mist-shrouded island of mystery in their midst.

Going back to her desk, she looked out at the little flakes still coming down, wondering how things were going with Cam. They'd had a guest with chest pains up at the Manor, and he hadn't checked in since he'd left to examine her. The good news was that she hadn't heard a rescue helicopter flying in, and nor had he called to tell her to prepare one of the beds upstairs.

Another bit of good news was that the backup medical team was on duty that night, so she and Cam could spend some uninterrupted time together. He'd suggested Angus Stewart's fir forest and she'd agreed, although staying in was appealing too. She was determined to spend as much quality time with Cam as possible, and they could talk freely when they were alone. Not to mention be intimate.

The burn he'd gone to look at the night before had turned out to be minor, but he'd still been annoyed when he got back.

"That family are the one problem this year,"

he'd complained. "We usually have at least one, but these people take the cake. I read them the riot act, as politely as I could, but if they don't shape up I'm asking them to leave. Gillian's so fed up she said she'd refund them their money just to be rid of them."

Harmony had commiserated, having seen the family in action at the fair. The two boys had relentlessly heckled one of the performers, while the parents had stood by, beers in hand, as though nothing was going on.

After that she'd taken Cam to bed, warming his chilled flesh with her own, loving him until he'd turned the tables on her, taking her to heights of pleasure she'd thought were only fantasies dreamt up by authors.

Cam MacRurie definitely knew his way around a woman's body—or at least around hers—but for her it wasn't all about the sex, and that was worrisome. Yes, it was definitely worth it—having a man who could give her intense, mind-blowing orgasms—but the flipside was the sense of closeness she felt with him, the comfort and emotional attachment that was beginning to grow. At least on her side.

In her head she knew he wasn't the man for

her. In a short time the Winter Festival would be over and Cam would be going on his next adventure. Maybe even trying that insane winged suit freefall thing. Just the sight of it had made her blood run cold and then boil with anger. Knowing he endangered his life with those types of activities made her want to smack him silly.

She was totally convinced there was no place in her life for a man like that. All she had to do was keep reminding her heart of it and everything would work out fine.

Checking the time, she called her mum, who was probably about to get ready for work. Although Delilah Kinkaid had enough seniority to request one shift and stick to it, she still rotated with the rest of the nurses.

"Hello, love."

Her mother sounded bright, chipper in a way she hadn't in a while, and it made Harmony smile.

"Hi, Mum. It's snowing here."

"Ha! We've had rain, and they're saying that's probably all we'll get before Christmas."

"Yuck," Harmony replied, although up until

today Eilean Rurie had been similar. "Are you looking forward to your vacation?"

"More so than ever," Mum answered.

She must be having a rough time at work to be so enthused.

"Day after tomorrow is my last shift, and then I'm off for two whole weeks."

"Good for you."

But, even understanding why her mum had chosen to go to Yorkshire, and not being in London herself, it still made Harmony sad to know they wouldn't be together at Christmas.

Snapping herself out of self-pity mode, she asked, "How's Fred?"

And then she got a good laugh, hearing about her mum making him take her to the ballet, after being given tickets by a friend who'd broken her leg and couldn't go. Her mum, like Gran before her, was a born storyteller, and the tale was all the funnier for her going back and forth between English and patois, interjecting Jamaican phrases into the conversation.

By the time they hung up Harmony was still chuckling, and over her brief lapse into the doldrums.

Cam came in just then, knocking the snow

off his boots at the door, those amazing eyes trained on her the entire time.

"You were talking to your mum? How is she?"

Surprised, since he'd come in after she'd hung up, she asked, "She's fine—sounded much more cheerful. But how did you know I was talking to her?"

"You have a special glow after your calls with her." He went past her desk, his hands full with his medical bag and the portable EKG machine. "It's obvious how close the two of you are."

Harmony got up and followed Cam into the medical store room, talking as she went. "We *are* really close. It still feels weird to know we won't be together at Christmas, but I guess that's how life's supposed to go." Not wanting to fall back into depressing thoughts, she asked, "How's the patient?"

"No signs of myocardial infarction, and she's feeling a lot better, but I suggested she get her gall bladder function checked when she goes home, and in the meantime stick to foods she knows don't give her indigestion. Turns out she has a lot of food allergies."

He'd stored the EKG machine away while he

spoke, and when he turned around and tugged Harmony into his arms she squeaked, surprised by the swift move. But as soon as she was in his arms she melted, her muscles going pliant, her heart-rate kicking up.

"Looking forward to tonight?" he asked, in between feathering kisses across her cheek.

"Mmm-hmm…" She sighed, tipping her head to the side so those talented lips could find her throat.

"Good," he murmured against her neck, making goosebumps fire up and down her back and arms, and her nipples tighten to ultra-sensitive peaks. "I thought we could have dinner at the Manor after, and you could stay over."

She stiffened, and he leaned back so he could see her face. When he lifted a finger to stroke between her brows she knew she'd been frowning.

His voice gentle, he said, "I thought we agreed it didn't make sense to hide our relationship? Have you changed your mind?"

She'd made a point not to go up to the Manor, and had never seen his part of it—all in an attempt to maintain at least a modicum of distance from the rest of his life. Yet she had agreed there was no need for the discretion they'd tried to maintain to this point, and refusing to go with him, to sleep in his bed for a change, seemed silly.

But she was still unsure. Did this signal a change in their relationship? A new facet that could add more complexity to the situation?

The expression on his face—so serious, almost hurt—had her pushing her reservations aside. And when she replied, "Knee-jerk reaction, I guess. Of course I'll go," his smile made her heart sing.

Cam forced himself to let Harmony go and guided her back to the main part of the office. He had a patient coming in at three o'clock, and she was due to go and do her wellness check on Delores Jacobson as soon as she'd checked that patient in.

He was tired. Run off his feet by the festival. But he was enjoying it more than ever before. Somehow having Harmony to share it with had brought back the joy of it, which had been lacking these last couple of years.

From the reception area he heard Harmony

start singing along with the Christmas song playing on the audio system, and he leaned back, smiling.

How different she was from when he'd first started playing them, when her lips had pursed, her brows coming together in that frown of hers. He'd picked music she'd mentioned that her gran had liked—not because he wanted to remind her of her sorrows, but because he truly felt hearing those songs, remembering the good times, would help her heal. Maybe he'd got it right.

Suddenly noticing both the box on his desk and the mouthwatering scent coming from it, he called, "Harmony, what's this on my desk?"

The singing stopped and she came to stand in the doorway. "I don't know. Katherine dropped it off—said that Dora asked her to."

"Oh." He was itching to open it, but instead swiveled in his chair to put it on the shelf behind him. "I'll have to take it up to the Manor before we go out."

"What is it?" she asked.

"Just some baked goods for..."

Damn it. He'd been about to say they were

for dinner that evening at the Manor but he'd invited her to eat there tonight, and he didn't want her to see what was in the package. Not yet.

Thinking quickly, he said, "For one of the guests. Dora promised to make something specific for him as a special commission."

"Okay." Her face fell. "I was hoping they were for you and I could share. That scent takes me back to my mum's kitchen."

"Sorry," he said. "Maybe we can ask Dora to make you some."

"What are they?"

"No clue," he answered, trying his best to look innocent, and not sure he'd achieved it when those little lines came and went between her brows.

Luckily, just then he heard the front door open, and Harmony went to greet his patient and check her in.

She left to see Delores while Carmen Henriques was still with him, and after seeing the young mother and her baby to the door he rushed back to open the box full of pastries.

The gizzadas looked just like the ones he'd

seen online, but just to be sure he pulled up the page with the pictures and the recipe again.

Gizzada—also called Pinch-Me-Round, because of the way the shortcrust pastry is pinched to create the free-form tart base— is a Jamaican delicacy.

The filling of grated sweetened coconut, spiced with nutmeg, vanilla and a hint of ginger, has a soft consistency, in contrast to the firm yet flaky shell.

Okay, he'd have to see if Dora had managed to capture the taste, as well as the look.

"Oh, yes!" Cam mumbled through a mouthful of deliciousness. Even if Dora hadn't perfectly captured the Jamaican flavor, she'd definitely created something absolutely mouthwatering.

Hopefully Harmony would like the gizzadas, along with his other surprises, when Doris made them again on Christmas Eve.

Early on, he'd realized his main mission that year would be to make sure Harmony enjoyed Christmas and found again the joy the season could bring. But he'd had no idea how to go about it until inspiration had struck.

If they could incorporate some of the things

she'd said she missed about the holidays into the Winter Festival, maybe it would not only soften her grief, but make her feel a part of everything.

Dora had been incensed, saying it was far too late to add anything more to the plethora of activities and tasks each of them had taken on. In the end he'd had to compromise, agreeing that they'd add some Jamaican treats and traditions into the Christmas Eve celebration, which would give them enough time to sort things out.

Since then Cam had been inundated with calls, mostly complaining about the difficulty in finding ingredients, but as always the CI's seemed to be coming through for him.

As he ate the last of the gizzadas, so as to leave no evidence for Harmony to find, he realized his obsession with Harmony was overtaking his life.

Part of him rebelled at the thought. Another wondered if it were so bad. Before long she'd be gone, and he'd be back to his happy, carefree life.

Somehow thinking that didn't make him feel any better.

CHAPTER FOURTEEN

ANGUS'S FARM WAS crowded when Cam and Harmony arrived, but with almost an acre of fields turned into a fantastical tree maze there was more than enough room for everyone. And because they'd waited, opting for a late dinner at the Manor, by the time they got there most of the families with little ones getting cranky and needing to be fed were getting ready to leave.

The temperature had fallen with the passing of the cloud cover, and snow still lay glistening on the branches, although it had been mostly trampled away underfoot. It gave the already beautiful scene a sublime sparkle, and Harmony felt her spirits soar just looking at it.

Angus waved them through the makeshift turnstile with a grin. "Good to see you, Laird and Lady. Enjoy your ramble."

Harmony blushed to hear herself described that way, but thankfully she was too bundled up for it to be noticeable. And when Cam took her gloved hand in his she was tempted to tug it away again, but restrained herself.

"Are you warm enough?" he asked.

"Yes, thank you," she replied, sounding rather prim even to her own ears.

But her stiffness evaporated under the spell of the tree maze.

It was like walking through a fairytale, and all the children seemed to feel it. Although some of them ran hither and yon, it was with the joyous abandon of puppies, and with a minimum of noise, as though they instinctively knew that too much clamor would spoil the experience. Others were content to wander with their parents, looking at the lights, trying to find their way to the center.

The scent of the firs was divine, and even with the lights she could see constellations of stars in the cold, dark sky. Some of the trees had ornaments on them, adding to their beauty.

Cam released her hand to loop his arm over her shoulder, and being tucked up against his side perfected the experience.

They didn't talk much, just the occasional, "Oops, back we go," or, "Look at that," when a particularly beautiful tree came into view, and she appreciated the lack of chatter. There were some things in life best experienced in reverent quiet.

Angus had followed the theme of Love, so most of the decorated trees had heart ornaments on them, and one in particular caught and held her attention. The ornaments on it were all rustic hearts, made from wood, or wire, in old-fashioned fabrics such as gingham, or of tin.

It brought to mind the little red felt heart Cam had slipped into his pocket and made her wonder what he'd eventually done with it. Had he hung it on the tree at the Manor, where it had had pride of place for years? She was tempted to ask him about it, but didn't.

These last few days she'd found herself weighing the intimacy of everything she did, said, or asked, holding back as best she could, not wanting to open up any more to him than she already had. Nor to have him do the same with her, knowing it wouldn't take much for her to fall completely in love with Cam.

In many respects he was perfect: thoughtful, kind, respectful of her opinions and her wishes. His lack of arrogance was refreshing, especially since Harmony felt there was much he could be arrogant about. Being nominal Laird of Eilean Rurie could have certainly gone to his head, but it hadn't. There weren't that many men she knew who'd handle the situation as calmly and democratically as Cam did.

Heck, she'd worked with doctors who'd thought because of their profession they should be worshiped. Cam was both Laird *and* doctor, but he didn't put on airs because of it.

The laughter they shared was the icing on a rich and delicious cake. Even when they were making love it felt joyous, free and right. It was a whole new experience for her, and one she knew she'd miss terribly when it was all over.

And it would be over all too soon—because in the end Cam MacRurie was too scary a proposition. His daredevil ways, his need for a stronger and stronger adrenaline rush, would one day end in disaster, and she was determined not to be around to witness it. She'd had enough tragedy and upheaval in her life that she would not put herself into that kind of situation.

So, even if Cam were inclined to want her to stay longer, she'd have to say no and go back to London—even though Eilean Rurie had sneakily, quietly, snuck its way into her heart. Much as its Laird seemed set to do.

"Here we are," he said softly, breaking her out of her reverie as they rounded a corner to the center of the maze.

Harmony gasped, enchanted all over again. "How lovely!"

There was a gazebo entwined with greenery and thousands of fairy lights, red bows and hearts artistically placed throughout. It was a place to sit and dream, to soak in the spirit of Christmas.

Cam guided her forward to it, bringing her to a halt just beneath the first crossbeam.

"Look up," he said softly.

She did, and realized he'd stopped her under a kissing ball made of mistletoe.

"Cameron..." It was a warning, even as her heart beat a suddenly frantic tattoo against her ribs.

But he just smiled, and said, "Tradition can't be denied, Harmony. It's bad luck if you do."

"I've never heard that before—"

He stopped her protest with his lips, and she'd never been happier to be silenced, melting into his embrace, his kiss.

Yet it wasn't a passionate one. Instead there was a tenderness to it she almost couldn't bear. His closed lips moved over hers so sweetly it made her want to cry. If a kiss could be a prayer, or a benediction, this was what it would feel like.

Wanting nothing more than to sink into it and never have it end, instead she gently pulled away—just as a family came around the corner and the children's exclamations broke the mood.

A little dazed, she asked, "Where are these Cailleach logs you were telling me about?"

Anything not to think about how that chaste, glorious kiss had shaken her previously solid foundations.

"Over there." He pointed to where a lean-to had been set up to keep the wood dry.

Easing out of his arms, she went to investigate them, Cam following slowly behind. They were strangely beautiful, the faces roughly hewn, but with a haunting quality Harmony appreciated. Cailleach was portrayed on some as old, careworn—winter personified—in others as younger, yet still mature, with wisdom and promise in her knowing gaze.

"Angus and his sons carve them all through the year, but this year I wonder if they'll have enough," Cam murmured, as though also somehow under the spell of all those wooden eyes looking up at them. "Our visitor count is up tremendously."

She wasn't surprised. Everything about the Winter Festival had surpassed her expectations, and the residents of Eilean Rurie put their all into making it amazing and fun.

"Pick one," Cam said, then reached out and took the very one she'd had her eye on.

Harmony didn't tell him that, though. It was the kind of moment best left to pass unremarked, showing as it did another albeit small similarity between them. Another intersecting point.

After she'd made her choice, and Cam had picked a couple of rowan branches, they went back through the maze to the bonfire. There Harmony contemplated the reds, yellows and blues of the flames for a moment, feeling a sense of destiny mixed with melancholy taking over her spirit. Funny how before she'd come to the island she'd considered herself supremely practical—all business. But here she was discovering new depths of emotion, a strange connectivity.

She smoothed her fingers over her Cailleach's face, and then tossed the small log into the flames. The knowing gaze seemed to glow for a moment, and then it was consumed.

Perhaps it was the beauty of the night, or the sense of having undergone a kind of spiritual shaking, but Harmony was left feeling on edge. As though the Cailleach had tried to warn her that not all efforts to banish the darkness actually worked.

There was a commotion near the refreshment tent, and they both turned to look just as Angus came barreling through the crowd toward them.

"You're needed, Cam," he said, looking shaken, his eyes wide. "We have a medical emergency."

Cam rushed off with Angus, and Harmony took off at a run to the car, to fetch their medical bags, her heart hammering as she wondered what she'd find when she got back.

And ruing, just a little, the interruption of their peaceful, lovely night together.

The patient was a young boy, perhaps two or three, who was lying unresponsive in his mother's arms.

When Cam tried to take him from her she hugged him tighter, turning away and shouting, "No, don't touch him. Don't touch him!"

"I'm Dr. MacRurie—"

But the woman wasn't listening, just screaming and crying, clutching her son to her chest. Even with all that Cam could see the little boy's chest heaving as he obviously labored to get air into his lungs.

A quick look around didn't find anyone who looked as though they were with the woman, and Cam was momentarily at a loss as to how to proceed.

According to Angus, the woman had suddenly cried out, saying her son had collapsed. When Angus had looked at him it had appeared the little boy's face was exceptionally red, but he hadn't seen any sign of seizing. Angus's youngest daughter had epilepsy, so he was familiar with what seizures looked like, but until

Cam had a chance to examine the little boy he couldn't rule anything out.

Turning to Angus, who was hovering behind him, Cam said, "Call out the medical team. Tell them we need the ambulance, stat. And get me some warm blankets."

"Take him into the house if you can," Angus said, before hurrying away.

Cam stooped down close to the mother, trying to get her attention. "Your son needs medical attention. I'm a doctor. Let me help him."

But it was clear she wasn't listening. All she did was moan and rock back and forth.

Suddenly Harmony was there. Putting down the medical bags, she knelt in front of the woman and took her face between her palms.

"Shh..." she said. "Hush, now. We're here to help your son."

Surprisingly, the woman quieted, although she didn't release her convulsive grip on her child.

"What's his name?" Harmony asked, holding the mother's gaze.

"C-C-Cameron," she stuttered, tears still flowing down her cheeks.

"Well, would you believe me if I told you

that's Dr. MacRurie's name too? Let Cam take a look at your Cameron, okay?"

As she spoke Harmony released the woman's cheeks and slowly reached for the little boy. Cam held his breath, waiting to see if she'd succeed in getting the mother to surrender the child. In the back of his mind he knew the clock was ticking. Depending on what was going on with the little boy, time could very much be of the essence. The delay chafed.

There was a collective sigh of relief from the crowd that had gathered nearby when they saw Harmony ease the child from his mother's arms.

"Take him inside," Cam said. Then, to the mother, "Come with us."

He didn't wait to see if she complied, taking off after Harmony as she ran toward the nearby house.

Once inside, she lay the little boy on the kitchen table, swiftly beginning to unzip his little parka, undressing him so Cam could do a comprehensive examination.

"Appearance of urticaria on his face and neck," she said as she worked. "And angioedema of the lips. Some sign of urticarial spreading to the chest and arms."

Cam had out his stethoscope and was listening to the child's chest. "Dyspnea and wheezing present," he replied.

The mother had come in behind them, hoarse sobs breaking from her throat as she watched them.

"I'm going to check his tongue and throat," said Cam.

Harmony had already taken out a tongue depressor and silently handed it to him, before tilting young Cameron's head back so he could get a good view.

But there was little room in the poor little fellow's mouth. His tongue was swollen and Cam knew they had to act quickly.

"Epinephrine—point one mil," he said, and watched as Harmony found the auto-injector and dialed in the amount. When she handed it to him he quickly injected the little boy in his thigh. Then he balled up a blanket and elevated Cameron's legs.

"Do you want to give him a dose of diphenhydramine also?"

Cam shook his head. "Not yet."

He was watching little Cameron, listening once more with his stethoscope to see if the wheezing began to lessen. When it did, he took the stethoscope out of his ears and made another visual inspection, noting the rash was receding and that two bright brown eyes were now looking up at him in some dismay.

"Mum, come and reassure Cameron that everything is okay," he said, waving the mother over, hoping she wouldn't upset her son more than necessary—which no doubt would happen if she started wailing again.

He heard the sound of the ambulance coming and looked across at Harmony. She was stroking the little boy's hair, speaking to him and his mother in soft, soothing tones.

Cam touched the mother's arm lightly, and she turned tear-filled eyes his way. "Your son has suffered anaphylaxis," he explained. "A severe allergic reaction. Does he have any known allergies?"

"No. None," she said, her eyes widening.

"Do you remember him eating anything unusual just before he went down?"

She shook her head. "No… We went through the maze, and he was running around as usual.

We'd just come back to the tent and I was about to buy him something to eat when he collapsed."

"I think I might have an idea," Harmony said quietly.

When Cam looked at her she was holding up a tiny piece of fir.

"I did a mouth-sweep, just in case. This is what I found."

"Oh, Cameron!" his mother said, before breaking down into tears again.

CHAPTER FIFTEEN

THE NEXT FEW days were a blur of activity. With less than a week before the Christmas Eve Gala Cam was kept hopping, while Harmony held down the fort at the clinic. The medical team from the mainland, who usually alternated with Cam for the evening shift, was now put on call all day, in case Cam was on the other side of the island when someone needed attention.

For the most part, however, there wasn't much Harmony couldn't manage. There were some headaches, a few minor lacerations and some wonky tummies—usually from an over-consumption of sweets. Nothing else, thank goodness, as heart-stopping as the emergency at Angus's farm.

The weather had held, with the storm the meteorologists had earlier predicted blowing away to the north, but another one was due the next day, with wind and snow, followed by colder temperatures. Cam and all the organizers were rushing around, trying to secure the tents many of the vendors used to ensure the wind gusts didn't cause too much havoc.

She missed having Cam around all the time in the clinic, singing off-key, being annoyed because she'd rearranged some cupboard or filing system. Mind you, he'd been a lot better about those things once he'd realized she'd actually improved efficiency. When she'd first arrived she'd seen his instinctive protective reaction, but had forged ahead anyway.

Her next suggestion would be for a really decent computer system, but she had a feeling he'd balk when faced with hiring a data entry firm to deal with all the older records. Although, in reality, there weren't that many people in residence. She could probably manage to input the information herself, in between patients.

Harmony drew herself up, shaking her head at the thought. She wasn't going to be here long enough for that and, depending on the reliability and precision of his new hire, he might not want him or her to take on the job.

The one constant in this busy time was sharing the nights with Cam. Whether he picked her up and she stayed at the Manor, or he came and crashed in her apartment, they were together. It worried her how often she awoke in the night and reached out to touch him, as though needing the reassurance of his presence before being able to go back to sleep. Or how waking up in the mornings and having his arm around her gave her a sense of comfort and joy.

Good grief, now she was even starting to think in Christmas lyrics. And, worse, realizing it had created an earworm, so "God Rest Ye Merry, Gentlemen" played in her head on repeat for the rest of the day.

She was going to meet Cam up at the Manor that evening, but he called to let her know he was running a little late and would pick her up. For an instant she thought about telling him she'd stay alone in the apartment that night instead, but she felt a sense of the clock ticking the moments she'd have with him away.

Surely she could plan and execute a slow, steady withdrawal in January, leading up to her departure instead? So she agreed. And that night, as he made slow, lingering love to her, Harmony let the thought of leaving drift away, so as not to allow it to taint the pleasure of being in his arms.

The next morning she was in the kitchen, mixing the ingredients for quick pancakes together, when Cam came out of the bedroom, his diabetes kit in hand.

"Is that bacon I smell?" he asked, coming around to kiss the side of her neck. "Yum!"

She'd been up for a while, but knowing how busy he'd been had let him sleep awhile more.

"And pancakes to go with it. Won't take me more than a few minutes," she replied, just as his phone rang.

"Sounds amazing." He was already heading for the phone, which he'd left on the coffee table, and spoke over his shoulder. Picking it up, he answered, "Yes, Angus, what can I do for you?"

Then Harmony saw his face change, grow stern and angry, and when he let out a curse she instinctively turned off the flames under the half-cooked bacon and pushed the pan off the burner.

"I'll be right there," he said, putting down his kit and heading for the utility room behind the kitchen.

"What's going on?"

"Two children apparently went out to the old fishing village last night when the tide was out."

She went to stand in the doorway, watching him pull out his wetsuit and a bunch of harnesses with ropes attached.

"They must have fallen asleep in the old rescue station and by the time they woke up the tide was coming in. The older one made it back, but the younger is still out there. Angus says he's sure they were drinking."

"Did anyone call for the Coast Guard?" she asked, hoping to hear they had and that they were on their way. That Cam wouldn't have to do what she was sure he was planning to do.

"Yes, but it'll take them a while to get here. If the boys have been out all night they could have hypothermia, and we need to get that youngest one off there before the tide comes all the way in. It's the pair from Gillian Strom's place and the mother says the youngster's not a strong swimmer."

He was coming out, laden with gear, and she stepped back to give him room to put them down by the door. Then he took off at a run for the bedroom.

Harmony stood there, frozen for a moment, panic making her insides churn, fogging her brain. All she could think of was Cam going into the rough water which, raging with the tide and incoming storm, would suck him away. Every bit of her turned cold, as icy as the sea he was planning on fighting.

Then common sense took hold, and she hurried into the kitchen to grab a couple of protein bars and a bag of dried apricots she'd spied in the cupboard. Dropping them into her bag, she rushed back to the front hall to pull on her boots and jacket.

When Cam came out of the bedroom, she called out, "Take your levels before you go."

He didn't even look at her, just snapped, "I'm fine. Don't fuss."

"But—"

The look he gave her as he tugged on a jacket, made her turn to ice again. "There's no time and I'm fine. I don't need you to tell me what to do, Harmony."

As soon as the words had left his mouth Cam regretted them. Not just because what she was suggesting was wise, and the right thing to do, nor because it was a reminder he actually needed. No, it was the way Harmony's face paled, and her eyes widened and gleamed green with hurt.

Before he could say anything her face tightened, and her brows drew together as she said, "Don't be an ass, Cameron. You can't save anyone if you're in distress yourself. So I'll drive. You can take your levels and at least eat something. I've got a couple of protein bars and some dried fruit ready to go."

"You can't drive True Blue," he said, trying to figure out how to do what he needed to and still get out to the fishing village as quickly as possible.

Harmony just made a rude noise and pushed past him to grab his diabetes kit. At the door she picked up his medical bag, her bag, and his car keys. Then, as she went out, she said, "You're the one who's in such a damned hurry, so let's go."

By the time he got the gear stowed in the back of the vehicle she had it running. He'd heard her cursing under her breath as she tried to adjust the seat, which hadn't been moved in God only knew how long, but when he got in she was belted in and seemed ready. The determined look on her face would have amused him at any other time—but not today, with so much on the line.

Cam watched Harmony struggle for a moment with the clutch, which was stiff, and the gear lever, which was misaligned.

"I'll drive," he said, impatience taking over.

The look she sent him should have incinerated him on the spot, and without a word she slammed the vehicle into gear.

As they took off along the Manor driveway, Harmony blew the horn to get the early risers ambling around out of her way, and Cam fought his very real inclination to ignore the snacks on the seat between them and the kit on his lap.

She was right. And he knew it.

Who would be helped by his being stubborn and stupid about his disease the way he had been as a child, when he'd hide from his mother when he knew it was time to test his blood or eat a snack? She'd used to tell people he didn't like the needles, but that hadn't been true. What he had hated was the way her over-solicitous care had made him feel—as though he had no control, wasn't able to have a normal life.

He'd gotten past all that with his grandfather's help, but now he realized the residual effect of his early years clung to him like an old, foul coat. Yet in a flash he knew Harmony wasn't like that. She'd made no mention of his diabetes since the first day she'd found out—never asked about his levels, or whether it was time to take them. Instead she'd clearly taken his word that he knew how to manage the disease.

Grabbing one of the protein bars, he tore the wrapper open and stuffed half of it into his mouth. As he chewed, he debated the necessity of taking his levels, and decided getting some food into his system was more important. He rarely suffered the "dawn phenomena," when his blood sugar spiked on waking, and didn't see why it should happen today of all days.

He finished the rest of the bar before saying, "I'll test my levels before going into the water, okay?"

Cam wanted her to know he understood what she'd said, and that he agreed, but when she only grunted in reply he felt his heart sink. Exactly when her good graces had become so important to him Cam wasn't sure. Moreover, when she'd become such an integral and nec-

essary part of his life was an unknown too—
but she was just that.

He'd fallen for her—all the way. For her
charm and kindness, her spunky spirit and
practical nature. Even for the fear in her eyes
when she'd realized what he was about to do,
which showed her concern for him. All of it.

The knowledge stole his breath, making his
already racing heart skip a beat. The urge to
blurt it out to her almost overtook his common
sense, and he stuffed part of another bar into
his mouth to stop it coming out.

This wasn't the time or the place. Besides,
right now the distraction of thinking about what
he was going to do, and if there was any hope
for a deeper relationship, could be fatal. Pushing it all aside was one of the hardest thing he'd
ever do, but he tried anyway.

By the time they got to the shore near the old
fishing village he'd managed to eat both protein
bars and a handful of apricots, and he made an
effort to check how he felt. Sometimes he could
feel the subtle signals his body sent, telling him
his levels were high or low, but right then all he
could feel was the surge of adrenaline.

As they pulled up behind Angus's vehicle

he heard Harmony gasp—no doubt at her first sight of what they faced to rescue the boy.

Although the derelict rescue station was still above the waterline, waves were breaking high upon it, spray flying to the seaward side, water swirling and frothing in strong eddies on the landward.

Cam, from experience, knew the path to get from the shore to where the boy lay, curled on his side on what was left of the station, wouldn't be easy. Debris and obstacles stuck up through the sand the entire way, but it was a place he'd explored many times over the years, and he felt no trepidation about the rescue.

Angus came over as soon as they'd got out of the vehicle, and followed as Cam went to the back to get his wetsuit.

"Annie Howell was going out to tend her sheep when she saw the older one crawling out of the water and heard the younger one crying for help. Lucky for them she had phone signal and called me."

Cam was already stripping down to his briefs. "Why didn't she call me right off?" he asked. Even a few minutes could make the difference between the tide engulfing the child or not.

"I'm closer—and she thought we could use the boat and get him. Once I got here and realized the tide was too low I immediately called you. I sent the older boy back to Gillian's, where I understand he's puking his guts out in between fits of shivering. From the smell of him, he got into some whisky. He's a fairly good swimmer, his mum said, but his brother isn't—which is probably why he didn't try to make for shore with the older one."

"Damn it," Cam said. It had become even more imperative to get to the younger child now, who not only could be suffering from hypothermia but alcohol poisoning, as well. "Does anyone know how long they were out there?"

Angus shook his head. "The tide turned at three thirty this morning, and wouldn't have started covering the sandbar until about five. I'm thinking they spent the night out there—or at least went out after their parents were sleeping."

Cam was in his wetsuit, reaching for his gloves, when he felt a touch on his arm.

Harmony held out a lancet to prick his finger, her expression stern, unyielding. Without comment he stuck out his hand, and she collected the sample on the test paper, turning away to where she'd placed the glucometer on the car bumper.

Cam pulled out the harnesses and Angus helped him to unwrap them, the two men discussing the best way to rescue the boy. Harmony walked away with his kit and Cam knew, with a sense of relief, that meant his blood sugar levels were good.

From then on it was all business. Angus and his son Colin secured the lines, while Cam got into a life vest and one of the harnesses, attaching another set to a ring on the vest with a carabiner.

Once he'd checked everything was in place to his satisfaction, Cam said to Angus, "Make sure the Coast Guard helicopter is coming. I'm sending this child to Skye for treatment once he's on shore."

Then, with a quick look for Harmony, who was nowhere to be seen, he went into the water, all his concentration on avoiding getting swept away or gored by debris.

CHAPTER SIXTEEN

HARMONY WAS BACK at True Blue, getting out the warming blankets and anything else she thought they might need when Cam came back with the child. She'd not been able to just stand there and watch him go into the water. She had wanted to tell him not to, to wait for the Coast Guard, but knew it would have been no use.

Cameron MacRurie was not only a doctor intent on saving a patient, but the kind of man who thrived on pitting himself against nature. It would have been impossible to stop him.

Yet even as she told herself she wouldn't look Harmony couldn't help it, constantly checking over her shoulder to follow Cam's progress as she tossed a couple of towels onto the back seat, hoping they'd be needed. That the sea wouldn't swallow Cam whole.

She'd allowed him to tempt her into an affair which had now become so much more. It was her fault that the fear she felt for him was so overpowering—a byproduct of the feelings she'd let grow inside. For all she'd told herself it would be a fun fling, she now had to accept that the emotions she felt as she watched him battle the frothing tide had little to do with sex.

No. She'd let herself fall for him, even knowing where that would lead. There was no one to blame but herself.

Annie Howell came over and offered Harmony a steaming cup of coffee, which she took with thanks.

"Don't worry about the Laird," she said, using her chin to gesture toward the water. "He knows these waters better than almost anyone else, and he's trained in water rescue too. He wouldn't go in if he didn't think he could get to the bairn and bring him back safely."

Yes, he would, Harmony thought sourly. Even if he thought it too dangerous, he'd die trying.

She was still hurt by his reaction earlier, when she'd tried to get him to take his levels before they left the Manor. His response had been completely out of character, and over the top too. Yet her fear overrode all of that, leaving her shaken and cold.

There was a shout from the crowd around the

shore, and Harmony spun toward it in time to see Cam clinging with one hand to a piece of wood sticking out of the water, clearly fighting to keep from being swept away. When he grabbed it with his other hand and seemed to get his feet back under him she realized she could breathe again.

"Almost there now," Annie said in a calm voice, but Harmony heard the undercurrent of worry.

Cam was trailing a rope, which was secured to the shore, but even so, if the tide caught him and they had to drag him back, he could get injured.

He got to the platform and heaved himself up onto it. Harmony could see him examining the boy who, after a moment, struggled into a seated position. Cam put on the child's life jacket, attaching it to his own before swinging his feet over the side and pulling the child into his lap.

This was the dangerous part. Harmony could hear the child's screams of fear, saw his legs flailing as Cam pushed back into the water.

How he found the bottom was something Harmony didn't understand. She realized she had her fist tight to her mouth, her teeth digging into her knuckles, but she couldn't help it as she watched Cam's torturous, inch-by-inch progress back to shore. Angus and Colin, and Martin Harris, who'd arrived to help, kept the rope taut, winching it in.

Cam and his burden were near shore when Harmony was snapped out of her horrid fascination by the sound of an approaching helicopter. Picking up the warming blankets, she trotted down to the shoreline, so as to be there when Cam and the boy were heaved back onto dry land.

In the background she heard a commotion, but didn't pay it any mind, too intent on watching Cam make the last few agonizing steps through the breakers, and Angus wading in to help him carry the child up onto the shore.

Feigning a calm she didn't at all feel, Harmony rushed forward with the blankets as Cam unhooked the carabiner that was keeping the boy lashed to him. Quickly wrapping the child in the blanket, she held out her arms for him, but Angus was already carrying him toward where the helicopter team was coming along the road from where they'd landed. They had a stretcher with them, and Angus surrendered the child to them as Cam sank down onto the rough grass at the edge of the loch, panting.

Harmony draped the other blanket around his shoulders and he looked up to nod, give her a little smile. But she didn't have it in her to return it, her insides still churning with the tension engendered by what she'd just witnessed. She reached out to grip his shoulder, as though needing touch to reassure herself that he was there, still alive, in front of her, and he turned his head to kiss her fingers.

"That was a workout," he said, between gasps of air.

Harmony watched the rescue team going back up the road, the child's father with them. "What condition was he in?" she asked.

"Freezing cold, but with enough fight left in him to almost drown me on the way back," Cam answered, but his humor fell flat.

Angus came back over and stooped down beside Cam. "The Coast Guard is flying him to Skye and his dad is going with him."

"I'm going to go too," Cam answered. "Just to make sure he's okay. I should make a report, too, since we had to call out the rescue copter.

Do you have time to take me over, Angus? I can wait for the ferry if you can't."

"Get you home to warm up and let me know when you're ready. I'll have the boat waiting," Angus replied immediately.

That news seemed to give Cam back the energy he'd expended on the rescue, and he heaved himself to his feet to take off the harness and hand it to Martin, who was collecting up the equipment.

Harmony surreptitiously checked Cam out for injuries, dropping behind him a bit as he strode toward the car. Then she was beside him in a flash, her heart rushing as she grabbed his arm.

"You're hurt."

He sent her a sideways glance, the edge of his mouth kicking up in a slight grimace. "Yeah. Caught the edge of something when that rogue wave knocked me off my feet. Tore my wetsuit."

Harmony let go his arm, staring at him for a long moment before turning back toward the vehicle. Here she was, fretting because he'd cut open his calf, and he was worried about his damn wetsuit! She strode off, leaving him to follow.

Cam stood on the passenger side of the vehicle with Angus as Harmony got in and started True Blue, hoping that when she cranked up the heat the old girl wouldn't expire. Martin and Colin had brought the ropes and harnesses to stow in the back, and through the window Harmony saw Cam twist, as though looking at the laceration on his leg. She'd have offered to put a pad on it at least, until they got back to the Manor and she could examine it properly, but his reaction earlier made her reluctant.

He was the doctor, after all, she thought a little sourly. If he wanted a bandage on it he would do it himself.

Cam finally parted with Angus and got in, still in the wetsuit, and Harmony reached into the backseat for the towels she'd stowed there. Then she jammed the vehicle into gear and drove a little way down the road to turn around.

"Well, that went as well as could be expected," he said. "Although Angus believes the father may try to cause some problems. I'll have to see which way the wind is blowing when I get to Skye."

She was coming down off the frightening

high, suddenly exhausted, hardly able to think properly. All she could do was concentrate on not crashing True Blue on the narrow island roads.

"What kind of trouble?"

"Oh, he was quick to deny that his kids had been drinking, and he said something about how dangerous the old station was."

"But it's fenced off—and clearly marked with 'No Trespassing' signs." Outrage superseded her exhaustion for a moment and her fingers tightened around the steering wheel. "And how ungrateful could he be? When you went out there after that child...got injured rescuing him."

"Don't get upset," he said quietly. "I'll deal with whatever happens. And it's just a scratch, Harmony. I've gotten worse injuries doing far less important things."

No doubt he meant all his crazy pastimes. She didn't answer, knowing that to do so would probably precipitate a fight. One she had no business picking with him, since theirs wasn't that kind of relationship. Just because she'd realized she loved him it didn't mean she had the right to question his life choices—especially since she knew there was no happy ending for them.

Cam MacRurie was far too dangerous a proposition for her, and if she'd only thought that before, now, after watching him put himself in harm's way and get hurt doing it, she knew it for a fact.

"And," he added quietly, "I need to apologize for what happened earlier, when you told me to take my levels before we left. I was out of line, the way I reacted, and I'm sorry."

"There's no need—"

"There's every need, Harmony, especially as you were right and doing nothing more than looking out for me. I guess I'm just used to going my own way, doing my own thing, without anyone questioning me. And I saw how scared you were, knowing I was going to do a sea rescue."

"That's fine," she said, knowing she was being curt, but not knowing how else to react. The pain of loving him and knowing she could never trust him to keep himself safe was too much to deal with right now. The urge to rage at him was strong, but she had her pride, and that had her saying, "I never told you not to go after that boy, did I?"

"No, you didn't, and I appreciate it." He sighed, but the air stuttered out of his lungs, and her quick glance caught him shivering. "I've always been the adventurous type, even as a kid, but my mother had a hard time with the fact of my having diabetes, and did everything she could to curb anything she thought was too dangerous. My grandfather, by teaching me how to manage my disease, set me free, and once I was old enough I let rip at whatever caught my fancy. I love the exhilaration of pitting myself against nature, or even against my own limitations. It makes me feel alive."

She pulled up at his private entrance to the Manor and engaged the handbrake before switching off the ignition and turning to him. His teeth were chattering.

"Go inside, Cam. Let's get you warmed up."

He reached out from beneath the towel he'd draped over his shoulders to grip her wrist, arresting her as she was opening her door.

"I need to know that you understand why I snapped at you earlier and forgive me."

Knowing he wouldn't move until she answered, Harmony said, "Yes, I forgive you—but I can't promise not to say anything if a similar situation arises. It's the way I am, and I can't change that."

His look of relief was immediate, and he leaned over to press his chilled lips to hers.

"I'm not asking you to change, Harmony," he said, thankfully releasing her and reaching to let himself out of the vehicle. "I just need you to understand."

And she did understand—perhaps all too well.

After setting a lukewarm shower, and helping him out of the wetsuit so he could get in and warm up, she ruminated on his words. Everything he'd said echoed within her, bringing back conversations she'd had with her mother about her dad.

"I think he took risks to prove something to the army after they rejected him over his heart defect," her mum had said, and the sadness and anger in her voice was still fresh all these years later. "It were as though he was driven to go after that high of surviving when they told him he wasn't fit to do what they needed him to."

Her dad had driven race cars and motorcycles. Then he'd done skydiving, trying for lower and lower jumps, or longer freefalls. Eventually it had been climbing. He'd been working toward free-climbing when he'd died.

The friends her mum was still in contact with all called him by his old nickname "Risky Ricky" when they spoke about him, telling stories about his daredevil ways. Mum laughed along with them, but Harmony had seen the lingering pain in her eyes.

It wasn't hard to see the correlation between her father's need to prove himself and Cam's drive for adventure. Had his mother's overprotective behavior done the opposite of what she'd wanted? Pushed Cam to prove that, despite his diabetes, he could do whatever anyone else did, no matter how dangerous?

The whole situation was overwhelming and, coupled with the fright she'd just had, made her teary-eyed.

She couldn't go through what her mum had—didn't want to put herself in a situation where she lost the man she loved because of his recklessness and need for another adrenaline rush. It cemented her determination to distance herself from Cam as soon as possible, before leaving him became harder than it already was.

Somehow seeing that deep laceration on Cam's leg just made it worse. She wanted to dress it, to tell him compulsively to keep an eye on it, but held her tongue. He didn't want her fussing—he'd made that clear. So she just kept a weather eye on him while he took care of it himself, aching inside with the worry of infection and the slow healing so dangerous to diabetics.

Once he'd left to go to Skye, promising to let her know when he'd be back, she pulled out her laptop and started looking through job search sites, trying to find her replacement. Knowing that the sooner Cam hired someone new, the sooner she could leave.

CHAPTER SEVENTEEN

CAM STAYED ON Skye overnight, making sure the young boy was recovering from his ordeal and doing everything necessary to report the incident properly. It kept him busy, and he didn't get back to Eilean Rurie until the evening of December twenty-third.

The preparations for the Christmas Eve Gala were in high gear, with everyone rushing about trying to put the finishing touches to the church hall, where it would be held, but when Harmony had offered her help it had been refused.

"Too many people barging about in there as it is," Katherine had told her the afternoon after Cam had left for Skye, when she'd stopped by the clinic.

Although it was a Sunday, Harmony had opened up the clinic in case of emergency. After all, she hadn't had anything better to do with Cam gone.

"You're better off staying out of it."

"Whatever happened to 'many hands make light work'?" Harmony had asked, amused by the other woman's sour tone.

"That went out the window about three days ago," had been the crisp response. "If you really want to help, come by my place later and help me make clootie pudding."

Knowing the other woman's reputation for efficiency, Harmony hadn't bought it. "You don't really need my help, do you?"

"No, I don't—but I could use the company. I hate baking, but this year I ended up on the list to make the puddings and I don't want to. At least having company will make it less painful."

So she'd spent the evening at Katherine's, discovering much more about the other woman than she'd dreamed possible, considering how closemouthed Katherine usually was. She'd spoken about her childhood in Bristol, and how her father hadn't believed in education for women.

"I left home at sixteen, and put myself through university. He didn't understand my ability with numbers and thought I was wasting time and money becoming an accountant.

Apparently, I should have been married and having children instead."

It was toward the end of the evening. They'd finished cleaning up the kitchen and the puddings had been boiling. Wine had been poured and they'd settled into comfortable chairs in the living room.

"How on earth did you end up here?" Harmony had asked.

The last part of the story had been about some of the fun times the older woman had had, living in Southampton in the nineteen-seventies.

"I came here originally as bookkeeper at the Manor." She'd smiled slightly—a rueful twist of her lips. "I saw the ad in a newspaper and on a whim applied. I was adventurous back then, and I thought it would look good on my résumé too. I had an idea that one day I'd go to Australia to live, and I knew the more work experience I had, the better."

Harmony had believed she knew what had happened next. "You fell in love with the island and never left?"

Katherine had given her a sharp glance, and then looked down at her wine glass for a moment. "No," she'd replied, lifting her gaze to meet Harmony's. "I fell in love with the Laird."

Surprise had arrested Harmony's hand, so her wine glass hovered halfway to her lips.

"Not *your* Laird, of course," Katherine had continued. "The old Laird—Cameron's grandfather. He was a wonderful man, as handsome as could be, and I fell head over heels. He'd been a widower for a few years by then, and although everyone knew he was still grieving I thought eventually he'd be ready to move on."

She'd fallen silent, her gaze going to the fireplace, her eyes getting a faraway look, as though she were revisiting the past in her mind. Not knowing what to say, Harmony had waited, wondering how the story had turned out.

"He never did get there," Katherine said. "And I wasn't the type to throw myself at him—to let him know how I felt. Instead I just stayed, became his friend, did whatever I could to protect him and look after him. Sometimes… Sometimes I wonder if things would have been different if I'd told him…"

Before Harmony had been able to comment Katherine had stirred, her gaze sharpening. "Some men only have room in their hearts for one woman, and the old Laird was just that type. I still believe I would have had to leave out of embarrassment or a sense of self-preservation if he'd realized how I felt, and I'd rather have had all those years of friendship with him than not. Life is full of hard choices, and I stand by mine."

Knowing Katherine wouldn't want sympathy, Harmony had just nodded. But inside she'd ached for the other woman, who'd perhaps missed her chance at love because she'd not had the courage to say how she felt.

"I was here when Cameron came to live with his grandfather. The old Laird was so worried about him… Cameron was an angry young man, sullen and withdrawn."

"Cam?" Impossible to reconcile the man she knew with a description like that.

"Oh, yes. His grandfather asked me, 'If I don't help him what kind of life will he have?'"

"Cam said his grandfather set him free." Harmony hadn't wanted to go into what he'd said about his mother, but knew Katherine would appreciate the knowledge that Cam understood what his grand-da had done.

The other woman had smiled and nodded. "It

wasn't easy for Douglas. He of all people knew how dangerous Cameron's diabetes could be, but he was determined to help his grandson accept the disease and learn how to manage it. He fretted constantly as he watched Cameron gain confidence and become the rambunctious boy he was meant to be, but he knew he had to give the boy the independence he needed."

The conversation had stuck with Harmony, still running through her head later that night, as she'd lain in bed, unable to sleep.

Cam was independent because his grandfather, who'd loved him dearly, had helped to make him that way despite his own misgivings. Harmony wished she had that same strength of character, but she didn't, and knowing her own weakness made her cry.

She wished she could talk to her mum about it, but she wasn't in a place, mentally or emotionally, to do so. No doubt her mother would have a lot to say about the situation, and Harmony wasn't at all sure she wanted to hear her mother's input.

Everything in her strained both toward Cam and away from him, and she felt trapped in an internal tug of war.

He called her when he got off the ferry the next evening.

"I'm just heading home to shower and change. Come up in a while, okay?"

She thought it strange that he wouldn't just stop by so she could walk with him to the Manor, but agreed to go up in about an hour.

As she strolled up she found herself greeting people she'd come to know in the short time she'd been on the island. Although she'd lived in the same house in Stoke Newington most of her life, and had friends of long standing there, the sensation of belonging she felt on Eilean Rurie was different. Somehow knowing you depended on your neighbors the way everyone on the island had to made fitting in a bit easier.

Funny to think how she'd worried that she'd stick out like a sore thumb and have a miserable couple of months. The stereotype of small places being unfriendly and hard to assimilate into certainly didn't apply here. She'd been welcomed with open arms, and knew she'd miss it terribly when she left.

Slipping in through Cam's private entrance, she found the most delicious scent reaching her nostrils, and she inhaled deeply as she shrugged off her coat and toed off her boots.

"What are you making?" she asked, walking through from the entranceway into the kitchen.

"Sugar cookies," he replied, giving her a broad grin. "I promised to make some for the gala tomorrow, and I was worried I wouldn't get back in time to do it."

Harmony surveyed the unholy mess on the counter, the flour and sugar on the floor, and shook her head. "Not something you do often, I suspect."

He chuckled. "Never done it before, but I think I'm getting the hang of it. I was going to borrow cookie cutters from Dora, but ended up picking up some for myself on Skye. Are you going to just stand there, or are you going to help me?"

Harmony laughed, opening the cupboard and taking out his broom. "I'm going to sweep up that flour before one of us slips and falls—then I'll help."

He looked so adorable, with a gingham pinny tied around his waist and his hair still damp from his shower, her heart raced and her stomach fluttered. The whole concept of steeling herself against the love and attraction she felt toward him seemed laughable.

"How could anyone be this messy?" she teased as she swept up the flour and sugar.

Cam shrugged, stamping out another biscuit and dropping it on a baking sheet. "I'm a pretty decent cook, but this is my first foray into baking, so excuse me if I didn't realize the mixer would send half the ingredients flying if I cranked it up to the highest speed."

That made her giggle, and they teased back and forth as she helped him with the next batch.

"How're you planning to decorate them?" she asked, when the sheets were finally in the oven and Cam was rolling out the next block of dough.

His blank look had her laughing all over again.

"Decorate? I'm supposed to decorate them too?"

"Otherwise they'll be pretty boring," she replied, getting her amusement under control. "Do you have any food coloring? Oh, never mind—I'll just look."

"All the baking supplies are in the last cupboard," he said helpfully. "On the left-hand side."

She found some ancient food coloring and some plastic bags and, as Cam watched with interest, made some colored sugar to sprinkle on top of the biscuits.

When she'd finished it was time to take the first batch out, and she showed him how to make designs on the cookies with the sugar. Once the baking sheets had cooled they put the next batch on, and into the oven they went.

Cam picked up one of the first set of cookies and bit into it.

"Mmm…" he said, his eyebrows going up. "Not bad at all, if I might say so myself. Try it."

He moved closer to her, holding out the biscuit for her to bite, and something in his eyes made her heart leap. Obediently she took a bite, and nodded in satisfaction.

"Delicious," she said, after swallowing.

"Yes…" Cam agreed, but she knew he wasn't talking about the cookie.

His gaze was on her lips, his expression intent, and when he leaned in to kiss her Harmony melted just like the sweet confection had melted in her mouth.

"I missed you so much last night." His lips were against her cheek, his arms warm and strong around her waist. "I couldn't wait to get home to you."

She didn't reply, just cupped his cheeks and pulled his lips back to hers. She couldn't admit how much she'd missed him too. To do so would be too revealing, even as she felt the bonds tying her to him tighten.

Picking her up, he carried her to the living room and laid her down on the couch, kissing her again and again. Time slowed, became irrelevant, as kisses turned to caresses and Cam slowly stripped her of her clothes and her defenses. Saying no to his lovemaking never entered her mind. Instead she reveled in it, crying out with pleasure as he took her flying.

"You're so beautiful," he whispered, his face harsh with need.

"So are you," she said, the words coming from her soul.

And when they were ready and she straddled his body, taking him deep, the pleasure she derived wasn't just from the sensations of his body in hers, as amazing as those were. Her joy was deepened, widened, by seeing his ecstasy as she took him to the edge and they plunged over together.

They came back to earth with a bump as the smell of something burning permeated the room.

"The cookies!" Cam cried, levering her off him and setting her back down on the couch before taking off running for the kitchen.

Still on a high, Harmony found herself laughing so hard at the thumping and cursing coming from the other room she couldn't get up.

Cam stalked back into the living room and stood over her, glowering. "Funny, is it?"

"Hilarious," she replied, gasping for air, holding her aching sides.

He pounced, growling, and they wrestled back and forth, with Harmony still suffering fits of giggles and Cam trying hard not to join in but eventually succumbing.

Entwined, they let their laughter turn to gasps for air, and Harmony relaxed into his embrace, blissfully satiated. Unthinkingly happy.

When he went up on his elbows she opened sleepy eyes to look up at him. Cam's expression banished her lassitude—brought her to full and frightened awareness.

"Stay here with me, Harmony. I love you."

CHAPTER EIGHTEEN

HE HADN'T MEANT to blurt it out like that, but something in the moment, in having her in his arms right then, had made him say it.

Having accepted that his love for her was deep and true, he knew the yearning for her while he was on Skye had just cemented it in his heart. It wasn't just physical intimacy with Harmony. There was something between them that both soothed and excited his soul, that made his lonely heart whole.

Her look of shock didn't surprise him. After all, he'd surprised himself with his words, although they were heartfelt. What he wasn't prepared for was the strength and ferocity with which she pushed him away.

Rolling away almost had him falling off the couch, which would have added embarrassment to what was already beginning to feel like a very bad scene. Insult on top of injury, or the other way around.

"No, no, no…" She got up, turned her back on him, covered her face with her hands for a moment. "Oh, Cam. Why did you have to say that? Spoil everything."

"Because I mean it," he said, not sure whether to be angry or sad. "I love you. I want you to be with me always. What's so wrong about that?"

"I can't!" It was almost a moan, and when she turned to face him her face was pale, her eyes green and tragic. "It wouldn't work. I *can't.*"

Wanting to take her in his arms, but knowing she wouldn't want that, he stayed where he was, flattening his hands against the cushions beneath him to stop himself from reaching for her.

"Why wouldn't it work?" He had to ask—to make sense of what she was saying. Was he the only one who felt how right they were together? Was he alone in knowing that what they shared was deeper, truer than mere passion?

She lowered herself into an armchair, pulling a throw pillow from behind her to hug it, as though shielding her body from his view. Or using it as a barrier to separate them.

"I… I never told you about my dad, did I?"

What did that have to do with anything? he wondered, but just shook his head.

"Remember I said he had a heart defect and wasn't fit for the army? Well, after that it was as though he had to prove there was nothing wrong with him. He was a daredevil, Cam—like you. His friends called him 'Risky Ricky' because of how he behaved—never cautious, always going full tilt into whatever crazy thing he was doing. He was a man who'd try any ridiculous stunt or sport as long as it gave him an adrenaline rush. Car or motorcycle racing, skydiving, mountain-climbing—you name it, he did it."

Cam wanted to argue—to say he wasn't that way, didn't do any of the things he did in an effort to prove anything to anyone but because he loved the adventure. But she was crying, and he couldn't bear the sight. It clogged his throat, making it impossible for him to respond.

"Eventually it killed him, Cam. He wanted to free-climb, and he wasn't ready for it. Or maybe his heart finally gave out on him. No one knows for sure. All we know is he lost his grip on that cliff and fell to his death."

"Harmony. I'm so sorry."

She held up her hand, tears still falling, but her face had taken on an expression of determination, and the lines between her brows were more pronounced than he'd ever seen them.

"I don't need your sympathy, Cam. I just need you to understand. I was six when he died. My mother was left to raise me alone. It took her years—*years*—to get over his loss. The entire time I was growing up she wouldn't date, struggled on her own. Because of his selfish need to prove himself he deprived me of a father and Mum of a husband. I had to listen to my mother cry at nights, when she thought I was asleep—had to see my grandparents get old before their time because of the death of their son, whom they'd loved so much."

She took a deep, shuddering breath and wiped her hand over her face, trying to erase the tears.

"I can't risk going through that again, Cam. I know why you do what you do, and I know how addictive extreme sports can be, so I would never ask you to give them up. However, I can make the choice not to watch you do them. Not to put myself into a situation where one day you might leave and never come home. I'm not strong enough to handle that."

Her words struck him like a series of knife-blows, each lacerating his heart a bit more until it felt as though there was nothing left of it.

Yet even though the pain was extreme, made him nauseous, his first impulse was to tell her that she was right. He'd never give up doing what he wanted—no matter how dangerous. And that impulse told him more about himself than he wanted to know.

"I understand," he said; they were the only words he could find in the midst of the fog clouding his brain. "I truly do."

What else could he say as he watched the woman he loved get up and start putting on her clothes?

Suddenly keenly aware of his own nakedness, he got up to tug on his trousers, realizing his hands were shaking as he did so.

Harmony dressed without saying anything else, and he trailed her to the entranceway and watched her put on her boots and then her jacket. When she turned to face him her face was expressionless, but the green of her eyes told him everything he needed to know.

"I've written up a job advertisement for my position," she said, her voice flat. "With your permission I'll start sending it out to the agencies. Perhaps put an ad in the Glasgow newspapers, as well."

He nodded, and somehow found his voice, despite the ache spreading out from his chest, choking him. "Yes, of course. Thank you."

A little smile tipped the edges of her lips, but there was little amusement in it and the sight was another heart-blow.

"Polite to the last," she said softly. "You really are an amazing man, and one day a woman with a stouter heart than mine will be very, very lucky to have you."

But I only want you.

Before he could say it, beg or plead the way everything in him told him he should, she was gone, shutting the door quietly behind her.

Around her were the sparkle of lights, the beautiful melodies of Christmas songs, the laughter of children. All the sounds of joy and happiness. But Harmony wondered if she'd ever feel either again.

Everything in her wanted to go back, to say she didn't mean it, but she couldn't—just couldn't put herself through living with and loving Cam.

Not when she knew what that entailed. What the likely outcome would be.

Who would put themselves into a situation like that knowingly, willingly, as though tempting fate to destroy them by stealing the person they loved away?

Letting herself into the surgery, she trudged upstairs.

She'd never felt more alone.

The only person she could talk to, who she knew would understand, was her mother, and she was loath to disturb her on her vacation. They'd spoken a few times since she had gone to Yorkshire, and Harmony was happy to know she was enjoying herself and liked Fred's family. She'd sounded happier than she had in a long time, and Harmony didn't want to upset that.

Yet eventually she ended up calling, desperate to hear her mother's reassurance that she was doing the right thing. If anyone would agree with her stance it would be her mum.

She'd hardly said, "Hello," before her mother asked what was wrong.

Unable to hold it inside, she let the entire story go, telling her mum how she'd fallen for Cam, and how he wanted her to stay but she couldn't.

"He's just like Dad," she said, crying. "I can't bear the thought of going through what you did, Mum."

"If he's like your father, dear, you shouldn't be afraid."

Startled, considering all she'd told her mother about Cam's adventures, she asked, "What do you mean, Mum?"

"Well, the truth is that your father was a wonderful man—loving, caring, intelligent and, yes, adventurous. But it was that combination that drew me to him, and I knew what I was getting into when I married him."

Her mum took a deep breath—Harmony could hear it through the receiver.

"Your father might have felt he had something to prove, but I really think it was more a case that he knew he was on borrowed time and wanted to live his life to the fullest. However, he'd told me that climb would be his last. He wanted to be home more—for you and for me. He just never had the chance to make good on that promise."

Shocked by her mother's revelations, Harmony said, "You never told me that, Mum."

"It hurt too much to think of. I felt cheated and angry."

Sinking down onto the couch, Harmony tried to take in what her mother was saying, but she couldn't escape what was, for her, the bottom line.

"I don't think I can deal with it, Mum. The thought of him going off to do all those crazy things, perhaps never to return."

"That's something you have to decide—but don't let cowardice cheat you out of something beautiful," her mum said softly, and the sympathy in her voice was almost Harmony's undoing.

"I'm afraid, Mum. I love him so much, but I can't stand the thought of losing him because of some silly extreme sport."

"Harmony, think about this carefully. I loved your father, and I knew who and what he was when I married him. I went into it with my eyes open, although I never expected to lose him the way I did. I was young, and I thought we'd both live forever. But although it ended tragically I wouldn't change anything—not one moment of the time I spent with him. We were happy for the short time we were together, and that's what I clung to all those years when I mourned him, even through my anger. Plus, he'd given me you, and you and your Gran kept me going even on the days when I thought I couldn't put one foot in front of the other."

"Oh, Mum…" Harmony was crying again, but they weren't the wrenching, heartbroken tears she'd shed earlier. There was a softer quality to them—healing rather than hurting.

"Do what's right for you, darling. But don't let fear alone rule your life. Nothing is promised. No one knows what the next day will bring. You have to live fully, wholeheartedly, and hope and pray for the best. Don't trouble trouble, 'til trouble troubles you."

Hearing one of Gran's favorite sayings made Harmony chuckle, but coming as it did through her tears, it sounded more like a hiccup.

"I miss Gran so much," she said. "And I miss being with you right now."

"I miss her too. And you. I didn't think I could face Christmas if it wasn't for this trip with Fred to take my mind off how much we've lost this year, but without you here to celebrate with us it won't be complete."

They fell silent for a moment, with Harmony thinking how lucky she'd been to have her mum, and her gran, to raise her. Just like Cam with his grand-da, she wouldn't be the person she was today without them.

Then, ever practical, her mum said, "Do you want to leave the island? We'll be in Yorkshire for another week. You could join us and go back to London on the train when we leave."

Horrified at the thought of leaving Cam short-handed during this busy time, she said, "No, of course not. I won't leave until I've found a replacement. I won't let my personal issues interfere with my work. Besides, God alone knows what mess the surgery would be in if I did."

Her mum laughed softly, and said, "That's my girl—full of vinegar and Scotch Bonnet peppers. Now, have a good think about what I've said. I know you're not the type to take chances, but some chances in life are worth taking."

"Okay, Mum. Love you."

After they'd hung up Harmony sat for a while

thinking about everything. Talking to her mum had brought to mind her conversation with Katherine, and how she'd missed out on love perhaps out of fear of rejection and hurt. She contemplated it all until the headache pounding behind her tired eyes overtook her and she realized making any decisions was impossible.

After all, tomorrow is another day.

Another of Gran's sayings, culled from one of the old lady's favorite movies.

With the comforting words echoing in her brain, Harmony went to bed. And, although she hadn't thought it would happen, she fell into a deep and dreamless sleep.

CHAPTER NINETEEN

CAM WAS UP before first light next morning, finally giving up on his attempts to sleep. He'd tossed and turned the entire night, getting only snatches of shallow slumber, his brain refusing to shut down.

Very different from last evening, when he'd stood staring at the closed door and through a fog of pain and despair had been unable to form a coherent thought except for the hope that Harmony would come back.

Stumbling back to the living room, it had soon occurred to him to go after her. In the end it hadn't happened.

He'd been at war with himself—unable to understand how she could be so completely determined not to stay. At the same time at the back of his mind was the thought that it was better this way. If she couldn't accept him as he was, what hope was there for them to make a life together?

Those were the two thoughts in his muddled head until he'd lain down in bed. Then his brain had gone into the type of whirring overdrive that was incompatible with rest.

What she'd told him about her father made so many things he'd noticed before come into sharp focus. How scathing she'd been about the water jetpack, her reaction to the sky suit video. And it also made him appreciate how frightened she must have been watching him get into the water to rescue the boy stuck out in the old fishing village. Yet she hadn't tried to dissuade him from doing it—just done everything she could to make sure he was fit for the job, even in the face of his disagreeableness.

She was a woman worth giving up the world for and he knew it. What he *didn't* know—and this was the part that frightened him—was what kind of person he'd be if he gave up all the things he enjoyed for her. Would love turn to resentment as he watched his friends doing all the things he wished he could?

It seemed asinine to allow what were really just diversions to dictate his happiness, when true, lasting happiness was within reach. Especially as he wasn't planning to keep doing extreme sports forever. No matter how fit he kept himself, at some point he'd have to dial it back. And he'd always thought if he had children he'd definitely keep his activities to the less dangerous type.

Not that he considered what he did particularly dangerous. Walking across the street could be dangerous if you didn't pay attention to what you were doing, and he was meticulous in his preparations and research before doing anything.

But there was no getting around her fears, and he wasn't sure he could leave his adventures behind just yet.

He couldn't help wondering if it was even fair of him to ask her to see it from his point of view. In reality, they both had a point. Her fear was no less important than his drive to experience new things. To pit himself against his fears and test his abilities.

One thing was clear, however. The thought of losing her was haunting.

Would he ever get over her? He doubted it. He'd never been a big believer in love at first sight, or soul mates, but he remembered how he'd almost stumbled over his own feet the first time he saw her…how his heart had pounded. And every moment in her presence after that had just pulled him closer, made him fall harder.

If a friend had told him he'd proposed to a woman he'd only known for a few weeks Cam would have suggested slowing it down, making sure it wasn't just hormones. But here he was in love with Harmony, knowing in his heart that it was forever.

Cam sat on the edge of his bed, head in hands, wondering how to work it all out and finding no immediate answer.

He didn't want to face anyone, wished he could stay in with his thoughts, but tonight was the Christmas Eve Gala and he had so much to do. Hiding was impossible.

It was as he was leaving home to go to the church hall that a horrible thought struck him.

Suppose Harmony decided to leave today? The first ferry would be docking at eight. Did she plan to be on it when it left?

He pulled out his phone to call her, then realized it was still too early. Not that she was a late riser, but suddenly, after what had happened the day before, he wasn't comfortable calling her before office hours.

Of course, she might have taken off before office hours.

When he got down to the clinic he saw the apartment was dark and his heart sank—only for it to soar with relief when he looked back at the front of the building and realized she was already in the surgery.

So he called her, wanting to hear her voice, although he'd try to keep things businesslike.

"Hello?"

There was a cautious note to her voice and his heart ached to hear it. Even before they'd come to know each other well her confidence had shone through.

"Hey," he responded, wanting to ask if she was all right but not doing so. "I just wanted to let you know I'm over at the church hall if you need me for anything."

"Okay," she said, still stilted. "If I need you I'll call. But I know it's a busy day for you. The temporary medical team will be around, so I'll only bother you if it's an emergency."

"Right. Thanks."

He wanted to keep her on the line, and found

himself standing still on the street, no longer walking, his feet itching to turn and go to her, just to see her face.

But all he could say was "Talk to you later."

Forcing himself to continue on toward the church, he braced himself for the day. Time to put on a happy face, since he couldn't stand the thought of having to explain to anyone, especially the CIs, why he wasn't his usual self.

Dora was like a whirling dervish, dashing about and making sure everything was set up to her specifications. Cam soon made himself useful, and had to smile when he saw some of the decor. The CI's had taken his request to make Harmony feel included to heart. Hopefully she'd like it.

Cam left a couple of times, to deal with matters on other parts of the island, keeping himself as busy as possible. Yet his thoughts never strayed far from Harmony.

Back at the church hall that afternoon, Dora came over, finally looking pleased. "The caterers are set up and already at work, and we're finally finished with the decorations. How does it look?"

"Wonderful," Cam said honestly. "You've outdone yourselves this year."

"You like what we've done for Harmony?" Dora looked unsure. "Do you think *she'll* like it?"

"I'm sure she will," Cam replied, suddenly struck with the thought that if he wasn't careful Harmony might not even see it. She was just the type to withdraw into herself and not come to the gala at all. And that wouldn't do. "Can I put you in charge of making sure she gets here on time? I have to go down and greet the guests at the ferry."

To his disbelief, Dora didn't even look surprised. If anything, her smile widened. "I will. It's going to be our best Christmas Eve Gala ever."

Cam smiled with her, but inside he knew it wouldn't be for him. Nothing would be the best without Harmony.

All day, while treating a variety of minor medical issues, Harmony had wrestled with the question of whether she would go to the gala or not. She knew how busy the CIs had been preparing for it, and wanted to be supportive. But she wasn't sure she was ready to face Cam, and wondered if her being there would make him uncomfortable. It was clear he loved Christmas, and he had been so excited whenever he spoke about the gala she knew he was looking forward to it immensely.

She kept busy in between patients by going over the advertisement for her replacement compulsively, and yet never quite got around to hitting Send to the various job sites. And the entire time her mother's revelations about her father kept playing through her head.

No matter what she thought of Cam's adventurous nature, or the reasons he'd gotten involved with extreme and dangerous sports, he was a very responsible person. It was obvious in everything he did. There was nothing truly selfish about him, even considering his determination to do the things she was so afraid of. To him they were just activities he enjoyed. It might have started as a way to exert his independence, but it had become important to him for other reasons. She suspected it was a way to stretch himself, maybe blow off the stress of his career and keeping the island running and profitable.

No, the real problem was with her.

There didn't seem any way to get past her fear.

Every time she thought about the video he'd been watching, with those crazy people jumping off cliffs in just a flimsy suit, not even a parachute, her blood froze. She didn't think she could bear watching him go off, knowing that was what he was planning to do.

Yet the love she felt for him was so strong she wasn't sure how she would be able to walk away. Oh, she'd no doubt that she'd do it, if only for her own self-esteem. But what would life be like after that? She had no idea—knew only that it would be bleak.

The question of whether or not she'd go to the gala was answered with a call from Dora.

"Harmony, we'll be by to collect you at seven for the gala."

"Oh, I don't—"

"Seven," Dora interrupted, in her brook-no-nonsense tone, effectively cutting off any resistance Harmony might have tried to put up. "And don't be late."

She didn't even wait for Harmony to respond,

simply hung up, the conversation over as far as she was concerned.

And despite her heavy heart, and her misgivings about spoiling Cam's night by being there, Harmony did as ordered and was ready when the CIs arrived to collect her.

Without an extensive choice of wardrobe, she'd put on a red knit wrap dress she'd packed into her suitcase on a whim, and was happy that she had. Pairing it with knee-high boots that had small pointed heels—what she'd always thought of as her "witchy boots"—she knew that at least her feet and legs would be warm. It had been windy during the afternoon, as another snow squall came east off the sea, and there was the promise of snow in the air again.

She was shrugging into her coat when the ladies arrived, and even though she was used to their habit of talking over each other, Harmony sensed a special excitement in their rapid-fire chatter. Not to mention the way they surrounded her and whisked her out the door, as though they were afraid she'd change her mind.

"Wow!" she said as they walked through the small parking area in front of the church hall and she saw the usually rather prosaic building for the first time. "This looks amazing."

There was a series of arches set up along the path leading into the hall, all decorated with white and gold ornaments that twisted in the breeze, refracting the light from hundreds of tiny bulbs.

Pausing on the path, she was just admiring their handiwork as the first bits of snow started to fall, adding to the ambience, when Katherine said, "For goodness' sakes, let's go inside."

"What's the rush?" Harmony asked.

But none of them answered, just hustled her forward under the arches and into the building. In the vestibule they took off their coats, and Harmony followed the older ladies inside.

And came to a halt, her mouth falling open.

The hall looked lovely, but what immediately caught her eye was a tree covered in poinsettias, strategically placed so it was the first thing anyone entering the hall would see. Interspersed between the silk blooms were golden hearts.

The CIs were all watching for her reaction and Harmony felt her eyes sting as she looked at their hopeful faces.

"Did you do this for me?" she asked, her voice hitching.

"Well, Cam said you told him you always had poinsettias at Christmas, but we couldn't get enough plants in time, so unfortunately silk will have to do," Ingrid replied.

"It's beautiful!" she exclaimed, giving them all a round of hugs. "How sweet of you."

"Look at the tree skirt," Dora said. "Sela made it special."

Harmony went closer, then stooped down to get a better look.

"Jonkanoo!" she cried, as she recognized various figures from the traditional Jamaican Christmas bands, who dressed up and danced in the streets. "Sela, it's gorgeous."

"It certainly caught *my* eye. It's so much like the prints we have at home."

The voice came from behind her. It was one she recognized but couldn't believe she was hearing.

She looked up and had to put a hand on the ground to stop herself falling over. Then she was on her feet, rushing for a hug.

"Mum! Oh, Mum…" She pulled back, tears filling her eyes. "What are you doing here?"

"We were invited," Mum said, brushing Harmony's cheek with her hand.

"The Laird arranged it all," Dora said, with a suspicious little crackle in her throat.

Harmony suspected there wasn't a dry eye in their little group as she hugged her mother again, swinging her from side to side. Then she was hugging Fred, who was beaming from ear to ear, and she was introduced to his daughter, his son-in-law, his son and three grandchildren.

Yet, through it all, even with joy coursing through her heart, she was aware of one thing.

Cam wasn't there.

She knew because she kept looking for him—even when the CIs took her to show her the special dessert table, with gizzadas, sweet potato pone and Jamaican Christmas cake, the latter baked by her mother.

"How did you manage all this?" she kept saying, but the CIs just laughed and patted her shoulder.

Eventually the family group made their way toward the table reserved for them, but Harmony still couldn't see Cam anywhere.

"Did you meet Cam?" she asked her mother quietly.

"He met us at the ferry and took us up to the Manor. I haven't seen him since just before you came in, though."

Her mum's hand on Harmony's arm kept her in place for a moment.

"I think he's wonderful, Harmony. When he contacted me and asked if we'd come for Christmas I knew he was someone special. Selfless. The rooms he's putting us in should be making him money, not being given away, but he wanted you to be happy."

Then, with one long, meaningful look at her daughter, she let go and went to sit with Fred, leaving Harmony to chew on what she'd said.

CHAPTER TWENTY

THE SNOW WAS starting to come down harder, and the small, glittery flakes that had first fallen were replaced with bigger, fluffier ones. Cam brushed off the bench with his gloved hand, then sat facing Grand-Da's grave, looking up into the cloudy sky at the snow drifting earthward.

Every moment spent putting together the perfect Christmas Eve for Harmony had been worth it just to see the astonishment and happiness light up her face. He'd stood at the back of the room, out of the way, where he could watch her unfolding surprise and see her reaction, and his heart had soared when she'd hugged her mother, happy tears on her cheeks.

"I wish you could have seen it, Grand-Da. It was one of the most beautiful moments I've ever witnessed."

It had taken a lot of finagling and some downright deception to put it all together. When he'd first got the idea he'd been wary of calling Mrs. Kinkaid out of the blue and asking her if she would come to the island. After all, she didn't know him from a hole in the wall. Yet Harmony's mother had been gracious, and almost embarrassingly grateful for the opportunity. Cam thought she might even have been crying a little when he'd spoken with her the first time.

But he knew what it was like to go through the first Christmas after you'd lost someone seminal in your life, and both Harmony and her mother were facing that alone rather than together. The year he'd lost Grand-Da, Christmas hadn't held the same magic for him until his island family had rallied around. His parents and cousins had made the effort to come too, and having everyone together had rendered the season not just bearable, but a lovely tribute to the old man.

Shoving his hand into his pocket, he fingered the felt heart. He'd kept meaning to put it on the tree up at the Manor, but somehow had always ended up sticking it back into his coat pocket. It reminded him of Harmony—of the day he'd realized the attraction he felt was far stronger than he had ever imagined.

"That's what Christmas is supposed to be, right, Grand-Da?" he said into the cold, wintry night. "Family. Joy. Love."

"And you've done so much to make my Christmas perfect, Cam."

The snow had muffled her footsteps, so he hadn't heard her approach, and when he turned to look Harmony was standing just behind the bench.

"I thought I'd find you here," she continued, coming forward to sit beside him.

"Just a little visit with Grand-Da. Being out here helps me think."

He couldn't take his eyes off her beautiful, shining face. Her eyes sparkled brighter than any of the holiday lights, shining amber in the glow of the nearby streetlamp.

"Thank you." The words were simple, but behind them was a wealth of joy.

Cam shook his head. "I don't need your thanks, my love. Just to know you're happy is enough for me."

She reached out then, and took his hand. She wasn't wearing gloves, and instinctively he covered her fingers with his to keep them warm.

Harmony looked down at their hands, and

then back up at him. "I've never been happier, Cam. But it's not complete without you."

Something shifted inside him—a deep soul-shudder that brought with it the realization that he'd do anything—*anything*—to keep this woman in his life.

He took a deep breath, the cold air filling his lungs and seeming to blow all his previous doubts away. Reaching across, he took her other hand. When she placed it in his, his pounding heart felt a little lighter.

"I'll give it all up—the mountain-climbing, skydiving, caving, hang gliding, everything—if you love me. I never want to hurt you, or make you worry. If that's what it takes to have you with me forever, I'll do it. I don't want anyone but you."

Harmony shook her head, those darling little lines coming and going between her brows, and he felt his heart break once more, thinking she was rejecting him again.

"I don't need you to do that," she said quietly, her gaze intent on his. "It's part of who you are...your adventurous spirit. It might make me feel more secure if you stopped, but it wouldn't make you happy, and letting you live your best life is important to me."

"The very best life I could live is with you," he replied, meaning it more than he'd ever meant anything in his life before. "You're all that matters—all I really care about."

Her frown faded and she smiled then—a sweet curve of her lips that made his heart race a little faster.

"I'm not willing to let my fears keep me from being with you, no matter what you decide. Go dive off one of those mountains in that wing suit and enjoy yourself. I won't promise to be there to watch you, and I can't say I won't be scared until I have you back safe, but I know you're not reckless. I know how responsible you are, and that you'll be as careful as someone doing something like that can be. But I also know that if you gave it all up for me you might eventually resent me, and I couldn't bear that. So go off to Peru, or wherever else you want to, and I'll be here, waiting for you when you come home."

He knew then there was no way he was letting her go and he told her so.

"I want to settle down with you, have children with you, make new traditions and have the happiness only you can give me. All those sports and pastimes are fun, but they're nothing when compared to the thought of having you by my side for the rest of my life."

Her gaze searched his for a long moment, then she smiled, and he somehow knew it would all be okay.

"Are we always going to argue over who's right?" she asked, the mischief in her gaze lightening his mood. "Even when we're trying to give in to each other?"

"I suspect we will, love," he replied. "But I look forward to every spat."

The wind picked up, just for an instant, and the snow swirled as though dancing a jig across the ground. Cam thought for a moment that the creak of the trees was like Grand-Da's laugh.

"I have something for you," he said, not knowing where the thought came from, but feeling the rightness of it.

Letting go one of her hands, he reached into his pocket and pulled out the heart, holding it out to Harmony. She took it, releasing his other hand to trace the luckenbooth design. Then she pressed it over her own heart, and when she looked up there were tears in the corners of her eyes.

"Cameron MacRurie, are you giving me your heart, having already stolen mine?" Despite the quip, her voice was a little wobbly. "I promise to take good care of it."

He held out his arms and she slid into them, wrapping hers around his waist.

"You already had my heart, Nurse Kinkaid."

The wind faded slightly and Cam noticed for the first time the sounds of chatter and laughter from the hall, the holiday music borne on the breeze. It seemed to typify the happiness filling him to overflowing as he held Harmony close, felt her snuggle into his embrace.

"This is perfect, Cam." She was whispering, as though loath to speak too loudly lest the aura of peace and love surrounding them be broken. "I'll always remember this Christmas, this night, as the happiest of my life."

"To date, maybe?" he teased, thinking about all the days and nights to come, knowing the future was suddenly brighter than he'd ever imagined it could be.

She raised her head, brought her lips close to his, and said, "Definitely."

The temperature was dropping, and her mother was waiting in the hall. If he kissed her he might never want to stop. But resisting her lips was the hardest thing he'd ever done.

"We should go back inside," he muttered, sublimely aware of her breath against his face, the sweet, lush sensation of her body resting so perfectly on his. "Everyone will wonder where we are."

"No, they won't," she said, getting a millimeter closer, so he wasn't sure how there was actually still empty space between their mouths. "They're all smarter than that. Now, shut up, Dr. Laird, and kiss me."

So he did.

* * * * *

LET'S TALK
Romance

For exclusive extracts, competitions
and special offers, find us online:

f facebook.com/millsandboon

◯ @millsandboonuk

🐦 @millsandboon

Or get in touch on 0844 844 1351*

For all the latest titles coming soon,
visit millsandboon.co.uk/nextmonth

Want even more
ROMANCE?

Join our bookclub today!

'Mills & Boon books, the perfect way to escape for an hour or so.'

Miss W. Dyer

'Excellent service, promptly delivered and very good subscription choices.'

Miss A. Pearson

'You get fantastic special offers and the chance to get books before they hit the shops'

Mrs V. Hall

Visit millsandbook.co.uk/Bookclub and save on brand new books.

MILLS & BOON